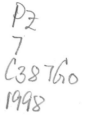

Good Idea Gone Bad

Lesley Choyce

Formac Publishing Company Limited
Halifax, Nova Scotia
1998

Canadian Cataloguing in Publication

Choyce, Lesley, 1951-
  Good idea gone bad

ISBN 0-88780-470-5

I. Title
PS8555.H668G6 1998 jC813'.54 C98950168-X
PZ7. C448Go   1998

Formac Publishing Company Ltd.
5502 Atlantic Street,
Halifax, N.S.
B3H 1G4

Distributed in the United States by: Orca Book Publishers,
P.O. Box 468
Custer, WA USA
98240-0468

Print and bound in Canada

Contents

1

Running for Darkness

Let me tell you about the night we pounded that kid Stephen. He had it coming so you couldn't say it was our fault or anything. At least that's the way I saw it then. People like that, I figured, shouldn't even be allowed on the streets, if you know what I mean. I didn't know much about him. Hey, you'd never catch me hanging out with anyone like that fruit loop.

Anyway, it was one of those nights, right? No action, no music, nothing happening. Ever since my old band, Jamwart Backblast, broke up, I was finding it a lot harder to keep myself entertained. I mean, it used to be fine as long as I could bash — I'm a drummer, see? We played heavy axe metal tunes. We played loud, and we played like murder. Whole neighbourhoods moved out when we practised cover tunes from Megadeath, Burnt Coffins, Vile Willy or even some of our own stuff. But that was all over thanks to the fact that we could never get along for more than two practices without somebody getting into a fight. It was all good fun, usually nothing more than seven or eight stitches apiece, but the equipment kept getting wrecked and we couldn't afford repairs. So Jamwart Backblast was dead and buried.

A drummer without a band is one lost dude. One lost dude leads to another, I guess, which is why I started hanging out with Dave, Lanker and Roach. Like me, these guys disliked boring scenes. If nothing was happening, we'd make it happen. Like that night in front of the library on Spring Garden Road.

It started out harmless enough. Roach suggested we have a contest to see who could hit the Winston Whatsisname statue with a big gob of spit from the farthest away. Mild entertainment, I admit. But it was cool because it grossed out a bunch of feminists who were walking by. Lanker missed his shot and nearly landed a wad on the back of one of the women. It splatted down on the sidewalk beside her, she turned and gave us all a look that said she thought we were disgusting. I smiled.

As a general rule, we hated feminists. How did we know these were feminists? I don't know. You could tell by the way they dressed, the way they talked and the way they looked at us. But the point is we didn't approve of feminists because they were always trying to change things. You know, mess things up for men.

Well, Lanker won the spitting contest but not before he "accidentally" caught some turkey in a suit with a big gob on the man's cheek. Buddy came after Lanker but then as soon as he saw Big Dave and me there too, he backed right off. Too bad 'cause we could have wasted him.

Like I say, it was a slow night. The batteries in my blaster were dead or I would have had it along. Nothing better than to blast it full-on in front of a place as lame as the library. But I had my drum sticks in my back pocket. They're good to have around for some practice or to shove up somebody's nose if need be. It was maybe nine o'clock at night. The moon was shining down on that great big goober that Lanker had planted on Winston Whatsisname's ass from maybe twenty feet away.

Dave was feeling creative so he kicked over the trash can and started to spread the contents around the lawn. Dave is not what you call friendly to the environment.

Of course, people were staring but they were all too wimped to actually confront us. That's how we knew when we were in control. People knew not to mess with us when we were in trashing mode. Anybody who did got injured. Especially if they were a geek or a fag, or something.

There was nothing much for me to do so I finished emptying the trash can, set it upside down and got out my sticks. Hey, I needed the practice. Ever since the death of Jamwart Backblast, my wrists were not as supple as they had been. It was a decent sound coming from the instrument and the boys started to groove with me. Roach gave it his best air guitar, trying to sound like Hendrix with his axe on fire. Lanker and Dave launched into singing their gross-out version of a goof song called "Nazis in Love." But these boys were not meant for musical stardom. Not a musical bone in their repulsive bodies. Still, it was noisy and it was obnoxious and we figured we were doing our public service for this dead-end waste-disposal town.

A couple of little geeks — seventh graders, I suspect — stopped to watch us. These little tweezer-brains thought we were cool. That in itself was pretty annoying. So we stopped.

Roach, who I think had some kind of merit badge in hassling little kids, asked them if they had any money.

"Pick on somebody your own size," I warned him.

"Shut up, Mick," he snapped and then turned back to the two little mutants. "You just watched the performance. You have to pay."

The kids were starting to move away.

"Not so fast," Dave said. Big Dave must have looked like a Saturday afternoon wrestling super-star hovering over them with his big hulk of nasti-ness.

The two little turkeys dug deep in their pockets and handed over a couple of bucks. Roach took the money and pushed them away.

"We let 'em off easy," he said. The Roachman had been wanting to be a bully ever since he was a little kid, but he was always too skinny to be a serious threat, until he got to be sixteen. Now he was still skinny but he had a really sinister look to him that made him as scary as Dave, who depended on size and sheer ugliness for his career.

The kids ran off down the street into the darkness. We knew they wouldn't tell a soul for fear we'd retaliate. But no harm was done. Chalk it up to education.

After that, Lanker, Dave and Roach took a break. They were sitting on the steps of the library when this guy, Stephen, showed up. I'd seen him around before on the streets playing guitar for spare change. That night it didn't matter if he could play well, he was just another fag. You could tell by the way he walked. I was still practising drums on the trash can when he stopped, pulled his hillbilly acoustic guitar out of the case and decided he was going to jam with me. Just what I needed.

I guess he was trying to be friendly but I figured with those kind of guys that was a really bad sign. I tried to ignore him but he must have thought he was in rock-and-roll heaven because he just kept playing away. It was pretty embarrassing, let me tell you.

My associates, however, must have seen this as a great opportunity for more entertainment.

"Put down the guitar," Lanker said, walking up behind him.

The kid tried to laugh. He didn't get the picture. I guess he thought he was going to just fit in with a bunch of good old boys like us as if it was hoedown night at the barn. Guess he'd made a bad call.

"Sure," he said finally, when he saw Dave and Lanker leaning over him and Roach breathing down his neck. He set his precious guitar back into the case. I noticed he had on a really neat watch with a big black leather band that had a skull and cross-bones on it.

"Who said you could be here?" Roach asked.

"Hey, sorry. I guess I'll just move on."

"Move on is right," I said. I didn't want to be seen with this guy. People might get the wrong idea. I figured I had an image to maintain.

"Not so fast." Dave had taken on his threatening pose, with his arms crossed like some hallway monitor from hell.

I could see that the time had come to get serious. I gave a good drum roll on the trash can. The fun was about to begin. "You play a mean guitar," I said to the kid sarcastically.

With that, Lanker knocked into the back of the kid's legs, making him topple. Dave got in the first punch before Roach pulled him away and said, "Let me at him."

Roach was still getting back for all the years he'd been beat up on the school yard, so he hit the hardest in the most sensitive places.

By now, Stephen was lying on the sidewalk but, like an idiot, he wasn't trying to cover his face. All we had to do was just stand there and get in some good kicks. Black army workboots with steel toes are excellent weapons for this sort of street cleaning.

"Imagine the gall of this loser trying to play music with a professional musician like yourself," Dave lectured me. I knew it was my signal.

The kid was already on the ground — grounded as we would say. He was already hurting, and I believed he deserved it for trying to hang out with us. Did I really need to take my turn at the festivities?

I decided I couldn't pass up the opportunity. My image had been tarnished. He had it coming. So I planted a solid kick straight into his gut and heard him let go with a choking, gurgling sound. Maybe he was spitting up blood.

The guys all laughed.

Then I realized there were people watching us from a distance. Somebody yelled to stop. I turned but couldn't get a fix on anything except a few shadowy figures. They must have been scared stiff of getting closer. I saw somebody out on Spring Garden Road waving his arms in the traffic.

A few seconds later, I heard the police siren. Dave broke into a big grin. Roach looked a little worried. Lanker wouldn't leave without a finale so he reached over, grabbed the kid's guitar and smashed it with a loud *carrong* on the sidewalk and then let out a hoot.

Lanker was already breaking into a run towards Grafton Street. Dave and Roach were hot behind him. I gave one last look at the sorry kid who was crumpled on the ground. I knew that I was gaining respect by being the last one to flee the scene. I was ready to give him one good last kick when he stuck up his arm to try to stop me.

The watch caught my eye. Yeah. I grabbed for it and ripped it off his wrist, nearly wrenching his arm out of its socket.

He tried to pull back, tried to say something but it wouldn't have mattered. It was going to be great little souvenir. I caught the look on his face — fear and pain all rolled into one. Maybe somebody else right then would have felt bad. But not me. I just smiled and ran like the devil to catch up with my buddies.

I knew we'd made our point and done a damn good job of it.

2

Cool Like Ice

I wore the watch to school next day. Every time Dave or one of the boys saw it, they just kind of smiled. I was feeling pretty good about myself when I ran into Dariana, the girl of my dreams.

There is no other girl in school like Dariana. She is like something out of my imagination: a real beauty but tough as tread on the front wheel of a Harley. She dresses a little bit like a biker although I don't think she has any biker friends. Dariana has problems at home. (Hey, who doesn't?) She'd lived on the street for a while but then ended up back home and back in school.

One time Mr. Lillman gave her a hard time over her opinions concerning condom machines in the washrooms. Lillman thought that school was no place to "promote promiscuity" — as he called it. Right in front of the class, Dariana gave this little speech about why condoms should be available in school. She ended by calling Lillman a "prunehead." What a babe!

Oh, the other thing about Dariana is that she sings and plays keyboard. Like me, she had lost her band. In her case it happened when she moved out of her house. By the time she came back home, her band, the Laminators, had found a new keyboard player as well as a new image and they were moving into top forty music.

Like I was saying, I was feeling pretty good about last night so I thought I should try to make use of my self-confidence. "Yo, Dariana," I said. "I'm still haunted by you."

She turned to look at me from behind her locker door. Her eyes were like cold, blue fire. "Haunted?"

"You know."

"I should take this as a compliment?"

"Yeah."

"Well then, thanks." She actually smiled at me, then slammed her locker door hard and began to walk away.

"Wait, I gotta tell you about what happened last night."

"I'm listening," she said as she was walking away from me at about ninety kilometres an hour. I ran to catch up.

I could tell that here was a woman worth the effort. Very cool. I'd have to really impress her if I wanted to make a play. So I cleared my throat and told her the story.

She listened with her eyes straight ahead as we walked. People parted as we made our way through the school. I was trying to make myself sound like some kind of hero for dealing with this fruitcake. I finished my story by saying, "I think we really made a statement."

Dariana stopped in her tracks. She looked dead at me with those gorgeous, angry eyes. "You're sick," she said. "Get out of my face." And then she disappeared into a classroom and slammed the door.

I was puzzled. *What's wrong with babes these days?* I asked myself. Forget Earth Science. I slinked off to the stairwell and sat down underneath the first-floor stairs to wait for her class to end. I felt like a wounded animal .

When the bell rang, I was there.

"What did I do wrong?" I asked her. "The guy had it coming."

"What are you? The judge and the executioner? Who made you God?"

The chick had a way with language. Nobody could put me down the way she did but, you know, I had to admit that I admired her for that. She wasn't afraid of me. She wasn't afraid of anybody. I wouldn't give up. Turn on the charm. Change the subject, I decided.

"How is your music going? Write any new songs?"

"Music's going good. I've been jamming with Alex," she said matter-of-factly. She could tell she wasn't going to shake me off. "Yeah, I wrote a new song. It's about not fitting in."

"I can relate to that."

"I thought you couldn't stand people who don't fit in, people who are different from you."

"Yeah, well that's different."

"Is it? Mick, how many brain cells do you figure you are operating on at any given time of the day. Five, maybe six, tops? You're a bigot, you're a racist, you're a sexist pig and you're a complete idiot who can't tolerate anybody who's different."

"So?"

"So it's the end of discussion."

Maybe I should have taken the brain cell thing as direct insult but I just figured this was Dariana's style. I was sure that deep down she really liked me. If I could only get her to spend some time with me, I knew we could iron out the wrinkles.

"I'll change," I said. The grin on my face must have given away my sincerity, though.

"Into what?"

"Anything you want me to be," I said, but I was giggling. "Wait. Don't walk away. Last time we talked, you promised we could do some music together some time."

"I lied."

"You can't do this to me. Look, I'm hungry. I haven't had a band for six months. I need inspiration and you are it. When can we get together?"

"I told you, I'm working on some stuff with Alex. I don't know if I'd have time."

"Alex is a dork."

"His IQ is probably double yours."

"So what does that give him, twelve brain cells?"

And that suddenly broke through. She laughed. Apparently she liked my joke.

"Who are you using for drums?" I asked.

"We run a drum machine through the keyboard. We don't need a drummer. Alex has one of the best rigs on the market."

It was the ultimate insult. "Oh, man, you can't be serious!"

Dariana could tell that she had hit a nerve. "You *do* have feelings."

I shrugged. What was a guy supposed to say to that?

"What's so important about a live drummer?"

"Well, music is supposed to having feeling, right?"

"Yeah."

"And a machine can't feel the music like me. When I play drums, I get *involved.*"

"I've heard you play. You're good."

I felt like a superstar. "I know."

"But you're not modest."

"I could be if you want me to be."

I was learning about babes. That last line did the trick.

"Would you be cool if I asked you over to jam with Alex and me?"

"Like ice."

"But would you be nice to Alex? He's an excellent guitar player, you know."

"I'll treat him with the highest respect," I lied. I hated kids like Alex — clean cut, good grades, student council. As far as I knew the guy could be a fag. I didn't like the way Dariana talked about this guy, but I knew I could probably make him look bad in front of her. I was talented at stuff like that. It was good that Dariana couldn't read my mind.

"Okay. If you promise to go very easy, we'll give it a try. Today after school in the garage at my house."

"I'll be there."

"Bring your drums."

"Oh yeah. That too."

3

Desperate for a Drummer

What a hassle. I had to pay Dwight Wayner ten bucks to haul my drum gear over to Dariana's garage. It was the last of my cash and I was feeling sorry for myself by the time we got there. I had just dragged everything out of Wayner's dweebcar — his Chevy Cavalier — when Alex arrived in an Audi, chauffeured by his mommy. It was a sicko scene seeing that little twerp and realizing his family had big fat bucks and that his mom did nothing but sit around and wait to haul her little Alex to band practice. I mean, what kind of music could a gorp like that play? It was going to be a bad scene, I knew it.

Alex and I were setting up in the garage, giving each other the evil eye, when Dariana walked in. She had on shredded pants and a tight top and I knew for sure that I was in love.

"Could we try to just find some common ground?" she asked.

"Yo."

"Remember I was telling you, Mick, about the tune about not fitting in? It's called 'Daredevil Difference.' "

"I remember."

"Here's the basic chord structure. Alex, give him the rhythm from the drum machine."

Alex clicked on the beat and it was pretty obvious. I got the point real quick and asked him to shut it off. "I'll see what I can do to give it a little more life," I said.

Alex scowled.

Dariana looked at us both. "One, two, three..."

Well, we were off and running. I started to bash away at my best metal beat. I was kind of loud so Alex had to crank up his amp and then Dariana had to turn up and I guess before you knew it we were all competing. I couldn't hear Dariana at all as she tried to sing but I was sure she'd be impressed with my work. I was as happy as a pig in deep smelly stuff.

When it was over, my ears were ringing pleasantly.

"It sucked," Alex said.

"Too much drums," Dariana said. "Got to tone it down."

Might as well ask me to live without breathing.

Then Alex started in on this lecture: "Mick, what Dariana is trying to say is that the drums need to fit in. They need to be part of the whole rhythmic pattern. You can't just hyper-exaggerate every beat. You need to temper the rhythm."

"What bleedin' planet had he come from?"

"Alex is right," Dariana said, ganging up on me. "Listen to the whole thing once — listen to it the way Alex and I have practised it."

I tucked my sticks in my armpits and sat back. I listened.

It was tight but bland. I tried to focus on the words — something about not fitting in anywhere, at school or with friends, or family. Stupid stuff. Who cares if you don't fit in?

"Way too mechanical," I said when they were finished. I was staring at Alex and his drum machine.

" 'Controlled' is the word," Alex tried to correct me. "We had *control* of the song. That's what you need in a tune if you want to make it commercial. It wasn't just noise."

Yah, right, Alex. The guy was such a gherkin. I picked up my sticks and hammered the floor tom just to drown out the little goon.

When I finished, he turned to Dariana. "I can't play with somebody this uncivilized."

I smashed one of my sticks down on the snare and let it go flying in the air. "You don't know squat about music," I told him.

Alex was putting his guitar down. "This is absurd."

Dariana was angry at both of us now. "Would you two stop acting like babies? What's wrong with you?"

"I can't get into this," Alex said. "We need a drummer, yeah. But not a Neanderthal."

17

That was it. I was out from behind my drums and ready to jam my other drumstick down this turkey's throat and use it to tear out his windpipe. Who did he think he was?

Suddenly Dariana was right in front of me. That cold, steely blue look in her eyes made me stop in my tracks. She walked me back to my seat, picked up the missing drumstick. Then she went over to Alex who was packing up his guitar. She picked it up and put it back in his hands.

"We're going to try this again. I want you both to bend a little. Compromise."

The word wasn't in my vocabulary.

"It's pointless," Alex said, but he was already hitting the first chord.

Dariana was staring past me. What else could I do? I gave her a beat. I found a pace that fit to what Alex was playing. A little too slow maybe, a little too controlled. It made me feel like I was playing underwater but I played. Amazingly we stayed together through the whole thing.

"Not bad," Dariana said afterwards.

"I didn't know that a guy like that could actually *play* real music," Alex said.

"A guy like what?" Dariana snapped back.

Alex went mute.

"I like the words a lot," I said. I hadn't been listening to them, but I knew Dariana would like to hear me say it.

"Thank you. Let's try it again."

We did it again and again until it was, well ... tight, musical, together. I tried a couple of little fancy things and they worked. It suddenly felt good to be playing real music with real musicians again.

Dariana was like a drill sergeant. After we played just the one song over and over, we jammed for a bit. Alex tried to impress me with some hot licks. I wouldn't admit it but the geek was pretty good. I tried to give him the beat to something really outrageously metal and he gave his axe a little overdrive. It was weak by my standards but it was a start.

"I don't care what kind of music we play," Dariana said, "as long as the song has real content ... not just empty words."

Content? Who cares? Nobody listens to lyrics. Everyone knows that. But I wasn't stupid enough to say that to Dariana out loud. I think all six of my brain cells were functioning just then.

By the time Alex's mom came back with the Audi, he and I had come to a kind of mutual stand-off. We had learned to put up with each other for two hours.

"I think I can talk Alex into you joining us," Dariana said to me after he was gone.

"What do you mean?"

"We're desperate for a drummer and he knows it. I think you might work out."

Now I felt like I had been manipulated. "What was this? An audition?"

"No. Remember, you invited yourself here."

"Yeah, I guess I did. So now you want me to play this *civilized* stuff with you two?" I was already shaking my head.

19

"Yeah."

"Oh," Oh boy, was she ever persuasive. "But it's not like what I'm used to. Too tame."

"I'll write some new tunes. I'll let you have some input."

"So sometimes I'll be able to bash ... the way I want to?"

"Sometimes."

"Cool."

4

Hogging All the Glory

I guess I didn't quite take the hint that it was time to leave but then I was in no hurry to get anywhere. I had no car (no driver's license, for that matter) to haul away my drums. So I was just *there*, you know. And *there* was a good place to be because Dariana was seeming more friendly. I guess she was beginning to appreciate my finer qualities.

Her mother stuck her head out of the back door. "Dariana, dinner time. Your father doesn't look like he's going to show up. Let's eat."

"Okay, Mom."

There was a second or two of awkward silence. The thought of food was like a light bulb inside my empty skull. "What's for dinner?" I asked.

"You wanna stay?"

It was only a half-hearted invite but that was good enough for me. I nodded. We went in the house where I got a pretty icy welcome from Dariana's mom.

"This is Mick," Dariana said against some pretty stiff competition from the TV. It was like soap opera wasteland in there. Food was steaming up on the table but Mom's eyes were glued to the pregnant babe who was crying on the tube. Mrs. Dubinski didn't even look up to acknowledge my presence.

Dariana grabbed an extra plate and put it on the table.

"Food looks good," I announced, trying to turn on the old Mickster charm and sweeten her mom up a bit.

"Mick doesn't speak in complete sentences, Mom," Dariana said. I think she was trying to be funny. I laughed at the joke. I've got this really well-practised kind of laugh where I snort in the back of my throat. Lanker calls it a killer laugh. D's mom just looked at me like I was mental.

I couldn't tell you what we ate. Something with rice, I think. I hate rice paddy chow — stuff that Pakis and gooks would eat — but I tried to put a good face on it.

"Good grub," I said, but Mom was about to burst into tears just as some greaseball guy on TV came in through the door where the pregnant babe was looking at her stomach. A real groaner. The commercials came up and Mom took a bite. I like them a lot. They are the only things really worth watching on TV.

"That's my favourite," I said to Dariana, pointing to the screen where they were advertising some new movie where this robot was shooting up people with a machine gun, chopping them right in half.

"Significant content," was all Dariana had to say. Man, conversation was tough around this place.

"Your father couldn't afford the time to eat with his family," Mrs. Dubinski announced. You could tell there were really bad vibes towards D's old man.

"He's probably pretty busy," Dariana said.

"Not likely," her Mom boomeranged back.

Time for me to stay out of the conversation. I shovelled rice paddy chow and tried to pretend it was good. The soaps were over and so were the commercials. Nothing on but news. Mom tried to turn it off but Dariana caught her hand. "Leave it. I'd like to watch."

"Kids shouldn't be watching stuff like that," Mrs. Dub told her, but Dariana flapped her hand in the air like she was waving away a fly.

My plate was empty and I was looking around for whatever, hoping maybe for a dessert or something with a little grease in it and then I see this reporter on TV. She's standing in front of the steps of the library right by the statue that we spit at all the time. There was garbage all over the place and it clicked: that was the junk I dumped out of the can so I could bang my sticks. I started to say something so that Dariana would make the connection, but she put her hand over my mouth.

"This was the scene late last night where a young man was beaten and kicked by a group of teens. It's just one of a number of recent assaults that have taken place in the city centre."

The camera jumped to a shot of a kid in a hospital bed. He had a couple of black and blue marks on his face. I recognized him — he was the one we thrashed last night. I was thinking, *whoa, this is cool. We, like, made the news.*

"Why do you think they picked on you?" the reporter asked.

"I don't know," he said. "All I did was pull out my guitar and play something."

I was thinking, *Stupid jerk. We picked on you because you acted like a fairy and deserved to get straightened out a bit. What's there to figure?*

"I know him," Dariana was saying, staring intently at the kid on the screen.

"What?" Mrs. Dub asked with a mouthful of food. She hadn't been paying attention.

"I know him. It's Stephen. He was friend of mine when I was on the street."

"Dariana, I don't want you talking about that in front of your friend."

The interview was ending. This Stephen geek was describing how we tried to teach him a lesson. Only he didn't put it that way. Then he held up his wrist. It too was all bruised. The hand had been scraped up pretty bad. "Some guy did that to steal my watch. He yanked it right off my wrist."

I was looking at the screen and gave a thumbs up in the air. Hey, this felt like a big moment for me. Nothing I'd ever taken part in had made it on the news.

Mrs. Dub wasn't watching me. "That's disgusting," she said to the TV. "What's this city coming to?"

But Dariana looked at me now. She was shocked because I was smiling. I guess I should have explained to her that the guy had it coming. How was I to know she and this guy had chummed around? Then she was staring at my wrist. I was wearing the watch.

"I don't believe this," Dariana said, shaking her head over her plate.

"And this is an artist's rendition of what one of the attacker's looked like," the reporter said. "If you know his whereabouts, you should inform Halifax City Police."

It was a pretty bad sketch that made me look a little too fat and a little too old. Nobody would recognize me from that. I was safe. What was everybody getting so upset about, anyway? Couldn't they see we were just doing a public service?

Dariana was freaking now but she couldn't quite bring herself to say anything with her mom present in the room.

"If they find the guy, they should just cut him up in little pieces and flush him down the toilet," Mrs. Dub said.

"I think I'll be going now," I announced. "Thanks for the chow."

I was up and moving out of there. Dariana's mom was still rattling on about what the world was coming to and who should get what kind of cutting up. Dariana followed me out the door and closed it behind her. Suddenly she was like a volcano.

"Get out of here, Mick!"

"What's the problem?"

"Just get out!"

Now I was mad. Here she invited me in for dinner like we were pretty tight and now suddenly she was screaming at me in her front yard. "What did I do wrong? I didn't do anything to you."

"Man, you are really thick. You just don't get it, do you?"

"That guy deserved what he got," I suddenly snapped. I didn't like anyone trying to lecture me. "If you knew him you must have known he was a fruit."

"So you beat on him just because he's not like you?"

"Look, you know that fags and weirdos and foreigners all get too much. They take away from the rest of us. Sometimes you have to put 'em in their place to let 'em know what the bottom line is."

"I don't believe you. Tell me, just what is the bottom line?"

I mean she was pushing me, pushing me too hard. I didn't need a lecture from some girl. Who was she to tell me my way of thinking was wrong? She'd never understand. Man, I felt so pissed off that I wanted to bust somebody right then and there. I took off out of there before I went out of control.

I couldn't believe that I let a babe make me feel so mad. I had to do something, right? Walking home I passed a little corner store run by a bunch of Lebanese people. I never trusted them because of the way they looked and the way they talked. A bunch of foreigners who came over here and took jobs away from people. I thought about maybe just bashing in the front window. It'd feel right good to do that. But there were people around on the street. There could have been some grief over it.

Then I saw this car parked behind the store; it was all silver, a nice set of wheels, a BMW yet — a real yupmobile. I was wondering how some dark-skinned guy who could hardly speak English made enough money to own it. Something wasn't right there. So I made my statement. I picked up a good jagged rock and I walked back up the alley, then scraped it across the hood leaving a long scar in the paint. For good luck, I took it and pounded once, hard on the metal until it made a little crater.

The back door of the store opened and the guy saw me. He started yelling in some foreign language. I thought maybe he'd come after me. That would have been sweet. But he didn't. He went back in to call the cops, I guess, and I just walked away as cool as could be.

After the tube news, I felt like I should return to the scene of the crime as they say and see if anyone would recognize me from the mugshot. Fat chance of that, really, so I was hoping to maybe just relive a few of those fond memories of last night.

Lanker was there hassling a couple of winos. I watched him from a distance before I went over to see what was up. When I saw that he was just joking around with the winos like they were all old friends, I didn't like it. After all, winos were just low-life scum. Better they should all be out of the way somewhere so we didn't have to look at them. I told Lanker so.

"Relax, Mick," he said.

But I wasn't relaxed. Ever since Dariana told me off, I felt like crud. Dave and Roach showed up just about then.

"We were on the news, dudes," Roach announced.

"*I* was on the news," I corrected him. "It was a drawing of me they showed."

"We were all in on it," Dave told me. "Don't try to hog the glory, Mick."

When you feel the way I was feeling then — ticked off, confused, angry — you're gonna lose your cool on someone. I guess Dave just happened to be the one in the way. "Dave, you're a complete and total idiot."

The two winos were looking at me now out of their bleary-eyed haze. Lanker and Roach were intent on watching how Dave was going to take it. Big, snarly Dave was always too gross and too ugly for his own good.

"Take it back," Dave said.

"Nah. It's just like you to try and take the credit when I'm the one who gets involved in the serious action."

"What do you want? You want this?" Dave showed me his fist. I stared at the bony white knuckles, at the scars and the three shiny rings.

I didn't know what I wanted. I hated the way I felt just then. I had a flash of that kid in the hospital bed. I saw Dariana's face swim up into my head. They had made me feel this way. It wasn't fair.

Dave was breathing hard, like a fat slobbering pig. For that alone, I should have busted him. It would have felt good.

"I take it back," I said, not meaning a word of it. "I don't know what got into me." That part was true.

Dave was still huffing as I walked away. "Apologize!" he demanded.

"Sorry," I said cynically, still not turning back to look at them. I threw my hands in the air. I didn't care if I ever saw those creeps again.

5

"Content, Man."

That next day at school, I felt like Dave and Roach were watching every move I made, everywhere I went. They had their eyes on me when Alex approached me in the cafeteria.

"I've decided I want you in the band," he said. It came as a real shock. "I think you add an interesting touch. I was watching some videos last night and I get it now. It looks good to have a drummer who plays it like a heavy, some guy who looks like an animal. It's an interesting image. But it will only work if you adjust to what Dariana and I are doing."

"How do I have to adjust?"

"We've got a goal here, you know. We want to make it. We want to produce something that is commercially viable."

"Bullshit."

"Not bullshit. We can do it. Dariana is a dynamite song writer. She can do anything. All three of us can create the right chemistry."

"Have you talked to her about me? Are you sure she wants me in the band?"

"She said so yesterday. She was trying to convince *me* to accept you."

"Ask her today."

"Well, I did," Alex admitted. "I don't know. She was just kind of moody. Maybe it's her old man or something. Don't take it personally."

"How come you're on my side?"

"I like you, man," Alex said. The words were less than sincere.

"Bullshit number two."

"I'm serious. We're different but that's what'll make us unique. It's the chemistry. That's what will make us good."

"You're desperate for a drummer," I translated. "And you know that I *am* good."

"Okay. Have it your way. We're desperate for a drummer and it's our time to move. We've been treading water for too long, Dariana and I."

"What about the *good* part."

"Okay. You're good, Mick. Whaddaya say?"

I could tell that Alex would be a really good salesman some day. Or maybe something worse — a lawyer or a politician. Mostly I wanted to get something going with Dariana. I wanted her to understand me. And I wanted to play music again. So why not?

"I'm in."

"I'll see what I can do to put Dariana in a better mood."

Dave and Roach couldn't understand why I was talking with the vice-president of the student council. Who could figure it? As I walked past them I thought I'd give them something to chew on. "He just wanted to consult me on a worry he had over school spirit. I told him we could boost the morale if they served beer instead of milk."

Nobody laughed. Dave eyed me with suspicion but Roach cracked that evil crooked smile — his trademark. I had them confused and that felt good. I also knew that I had stepped one foot over the line just by talking to Alex. I was in no man's land and wondered if I could ever go back.

After school, Dariana found *me*. "Come clear your drums out of my garage. I want them out of there. Today."

I thought I'd try a different approach. We'd had some harsh words. I knew better. You have to handle women with a certain kind of psychology so they think they are winning the battles. My old man taught me that. It was probably the only reasonable word of advice he ever gave me.

"Tell me about the street," I said, wanting to change the subject. "Tell me what it was like."

I caught her off guard. She turned her back on me like she was going to walk away but then she wheeled round. "Stephen is one of the few good people I knew there. He's gay. You're right about that. People pick on him for it. Guys like you. I've seen Stephen and his friends get trashed before — just for being who they are."

"It comes with the territory," I admitted.

"Why?"

"You know," I said, but I could see I was heading down Dead-End Alley again. Big mistake. "I wouldn't have beat on him if I had known he was your friend."

"Oh great," she said sarcastically. "I'll draw you up a list of all my friends so you won't beat on them. What about everybody else? Who you gonna grind into the dirt next?"

"I get over-excited sometimes," I tried to explain. "It's something that happens when I'm around guys like Dave and my other friends."

"You think you impress them by beating the stuffing out of strangers?"

I blinked. That was exactly the way it worked but I'd never admitted it to myself. I sure wasn't about to admit it to her. "Nah. I do it 'cause I have to." I swallowed hard and tried to pretend I felt sorry about it. "But it's different now. I'm changing."

"On the street, I knew other guys like you. They acted that way because they were hurting inside. Hurting bad. In that sense, they were just like me. Only I didn't have to send somebody to the hospital to make myself feel better."

She was looking at the watch again.

"If that guy was so down and out, how come he had something like this? Somebody paid big bucks for this beauty," I asked.

"Stephen was panhandling, playing in front of the line-up at the Palace one night. This guy came along. Turned out to be Eddie Van Halen

33

who was in town for a concert. Eddie liked the way Stephen played. He gave him the watch. It blew us all away."

"Too much." I looked at the watch on my wrist and thought it was pretty cool that it had once belonged to Eddie Van Halen.

"Stephen thought it was a good omen."

"What do you mean?"

"Like good luck. He wants to make it as a guitarist."

"Fat chance he has hanging out on street corners."

"Some people don't have many options."

"What about you? You had options. You went back home. How come?"

"Home sucks. My mother and father argue a lot when my old man comes home... which isn't often. The rest of the time, my mom watches soaps and tells me how messed up her life is. I thought my life was too, until I lived on the street. That was worse."

"I get the picture."

"I couldn't do what Stephen did. He played his music on the street. I couldn't do that with a keyboard. I didn't miss much about home except for the fact that it wasn't quite as dangerous as the street. And the music. I didn't have my keyboard. I wasn't writing songs. I felt really lost."

"I felt the same way when my band busted up. Lost."

"Alex wants you with us."

"I know. But you don't."

"I did."

"Before you found out about the thing in front of the library."

"Yeah."

"Maybe I'll grow out of it. That's what my mother says."

"You mean you're admitting that what you did was wrong?"

This was getting tricky. Dariana was looking for a big time confession. "I'm not always right, I guess."

Her eyes opened wide. "I don't believe I'm hearing this."

"Well, like that song of yours. I liked the words. They made sense."

"I thought content didn't matter. 'Nobody listens to words,' " she said, as if she had read my mind.

"That's what I mean. I was wrong. I listened. You were singing about what it feels like to always be on the outside. I know that feeling. I've been on the outside a lot." I wanted to go on and tell her about the line that had just been drawn between me and the guys but I figured I had already said too much.

"You'd be nothing but trouble if you were in our band."

I smiled and shook my head. "I'll try to be good," I said and suddenly felt a like a little boy making a promise. And for a split second there, looking at Dariana, I almost thought I was telling the truth. I'd do just about anything to be around her.

Session number two in Dariana's garage was a wild success. I tried real hard to be *good*, to be co-operative, and it paid off. I picked up quickly on about three of the tunes Dariana had written. They were tough, they had spirit and they had kick. It wasn't exactly bashing on a metal over-load tune but it was enough. The music felt good. The drums beneath my sticks felt like they were working on their own. Alex was beaming like a little kid as he picked through a series of serious licks with his distortion pedal to the limit. I bet you could hear us five blocks away at the Canadian Tire store.

"Okay, let's try this," Dariana said. "You know how they used to do protest songs in the old days?"

"Ah, c'mon," I groaned. "I'll do anything but folk music. Don't go sixties on me."

"No way. No sixties. This is now. But it is a protest song."

"What's the issue?" Alex asked.

"Condoms."

Alex looked puzzled.

"Alex, you know how the school board muzzled the student council for wanting to have condom machines installed in the school washrooms."

"We voted in favour of it. We just couldn't make them do it. They argued that kids shouldn't be having sex and that putting the machines in the

36

school would be promoting ... what was the word ... promiscuity."

"So?" I asked. "What is wrong with promiscuity?"

"So I wrote this. You'll love it, Mick. It's very angry, very loud. Play as loud as you want."

She ran through it once so I could hear the lyrics and she explained the chords to Alex.

"Don't you think it's just too limited in its appeal?" Alex asked. He didn't seem that keen on the song. "We should be thinking about a broader audience. This is just about a measly little school issue."

"But it's a real issue, Alex. I need to write songs about real issues. Things that matter."

"Content, man," I told Alex. "Dariana wants the words to mean something." I would be on her side for once. I still didn't care what she sang, as long as she sang it loud and sang it with punch. Condoms or condominiums, who cares?

Alex gave it up. "Is that an F after the A minor on the bridge?" he asked Dariana.

"D first, then A minor."

"Got it."

Three weak tries and then on the fourth time I found the right backbeat, hammered on the floor tom for the bridge and then piled on the wood for the end. Dariana was beaming. My ears were ringing. Music was making me deaf. How was I going to hear all the lyrics next time?

"We need a name for the band," Alex said. "We need something that fits."

It was some kind of commitment that we *were* in fact a band, not just a trio of goofballs making noise in a garage.

"Good idea," said Dariana. Another commitment. "But it can't sound too wimpy."

"I got it," I said. "Good Idea Gone Bad."

The name stuck like peanut butter to the roof of your mouth.

6

Gutless Musicians on the Road to Muzak

For a couple of weeks, music took over my life. We put in long hours practising in Dariana's garage. We recorded some of our stuff on her old man's tape recorder and it sounded pretty together.

I only ever saw her father once. He came home early from work one day and started yelling at Dariana.

"How come I can't park my car in my own garage?" he demanded.

"We're practising," D said. "We need the space. Who cares if your car sits outside?"

"I care," he said. "It's my garage." The guy looked like some kind of angry rooster.

I thought I could help out in the argument so I walked over.

"*What* is this?" dear old dad asked his little girl.

"*This* is my friend, Mick," she said.

I held out my hand but the dude just shook his head and walked off towards the house.

"I think you scared him," Alex said.

"I was just trying to be friendly."

Dariana's mom had begun to like me okay. I offered to take the trash out and stuff like that. So I thought I could also impress her old man into seeing that I was okay. Guess it didn't work.

"Don't mind him," Dariana said. "He was born with a bad temper."

A few minutes later I could hear him inside the house arguing with Dariana's mom.

"We better get back to work and make some noise to drown out the lovebirds so the neighbours won't hear," Dariana said.

Thanks to my drumming, the music was starting to have some real muscle. I persuaded Alex and Dariana to do a few old classics like "Don't Fear the Reaper" by Blue Oyster Cult and some Def Leppard tunes that were dear to my heart. But mostly we did original material that Dariana wrote, like "The Condom Song." And it was her songs that made life pretty interesting for GIGB.

Word reached us that the school was going to have a dance and a couple of the teachers, Mr. Alphonse and Mrs. James, were holding auditions to select the band that would be hired for the gig.

"No way," I said. "They'll never hire us in a million years."

"We should give it a shot," Alex insisted. "Look, they always hire bands from outside. If we get the gig, it would be the first time that kids from this school play for the dance."

"Oh, yeah, right. Just as long as no one listens to our lyrics," Dariana said.

"So, we don't play anything to offend them, that's all," Alex responded.

Dariana gave him a foul look.

"Mr. Alphonse likes me," Alex said. "I'm on student council, right?"

The little twerp had to remind me of this very upsetting fact. I slammed the high hat with my sticks. "Look, like I said, we won't get hired. They'll pick somebody like Lawrence Welk. They ain't gonna hire us. Let's just forget it."

Alex went bug-eyed and I felt like belting him just for being such a gorkwiener.

"I say we try out anyway," Dariana said. "What's wrong with that?"

"Just no controversial songs, right?" Alex said. "And no heavy bashing. We keep it real tight and real clean."

I dropped my sticks and held my hands in front of my face like I was about to pray. "I promise not to play anything that I wouldn't play in church," I said.

Out of the corner of my eye, I saw Dariana smile. I think my charm was starting to get through to her.

We learned a couple of cover tunes of top forty stuff. I went along for the ride. The two bands before us were older — guys in college, I think. The first band did fifties and sixties standards that made me want to toss my cookies. All clean-looking dinks in ties and polished shoes. My guess is they had been locked up in a time capsule and were just released after thirty years underground.

The next group had a little more zip. They called themselves the Emotional Rangers but they were pretty flat. They played nothing more than predictable tunes they churned out at gigs in downtown pubs.

One other alternative band failed to show, so that left us. Alphonse and James went out for coffee while we set up. About twenty kids had heard the music and sneaked into the auditorium. It was dark at the back and when the teachers returned, they didn't notice that we now had an audience. I felt a lot better about having some real humans in the room, instead of just teachers. I tightened down my drums. Alex and Dar got in tune and we were ready to rock.

We were very tame musicians through two songs and I knew we were doing okay because Alphonse hadn't told us to quit. We had one more tune to do. Alex said we should do our last top forty song — "Waiting out the Dawn." Real middle-of-the-road monotony, as far as I was concerned.

But, hey, you can only keep a pound of dynamite in a closet for so long before someone gives it a match. And I looked way in the back of the auditorium and saw some of the kids starting to leave. *Holy smokes*, I said to myself. We bored the little beggars. We were already over the hill before our career got off the ground.

I looked at Dariana. "We do 'The Condom Song,' " I said.

"No," she said. "Let's stick to the plan."

"Don't blow it now," Alex whispered to me, and hit the first chord to "Waiting."

I nodded to the back of the room. Dariana now saw the kids leaving. A couple of her friends were back there, I think, because now she saw what had become of us — a trio of wimped-out, gutless musicians on the road to Muzak.

We had to act quickly if we didn't want to lose our audience or even our reputation (before we even had one).

"One, two, three," I counted off and then — *slam*. I did the drum intro, setting up the backbeat for "The Condom Song." It was a kind of rap/reggae hip-hop thing with a twist of metal. Very original. Very loud. And full of meaningful lyrics. Alex had no choice but to go along since the song was already rolling down the highway.

The kids stopped dead in their tracks. Alphonse and James looked up from their coffees and stared at us like we had all just changed into werewolves before their very eyes. Dariana belted out the words loud and clear:

When there's problems that you just can't hide,
Don't cover it up, that's suicide.
No head in the sand, got to make a stand;
It's just a condom machine, not a lie routine —
Put your fears aside, let the kids decide,
let the people decide,
let us all decide.

43

Well, maybe there was some language even stronger than that but to Dariana, these were the words that mattered.

The song had so much pounding energy and anger that you could feel it in the air when we hit the final note and the kids in the back of the auditorium started to cheer. Alphonse turned around and shouted at them.

"You are not supposed to be in here. This is a closed session. Now leave immediately or I'll take down your names."

I had a sudden craving to zero in on the back of his head while he was turned around and launch a big gob of spit straight at that little bald spot that was suggesting itself as an all-too-perfect target. But I was trying to be good — for Dariana and for the band. Besides, I wasn't as skilled as, say, Roach who could have picked off a sparrow flying across the yard.

Instead, I sat quietly, waiting. Waiting for what? For somebody to say something, I guess.

Alex was mad, yes, but he was trying to be cool, trying to be Mr. Student Council. "Now we wouldn't be playing that song at the dance, Mr. Alphonse. We just want to let you see that we have ... range in our music. We're very versatile."

"I'm sure you are, Alex," Mrs. James interjected. "But we feel that the, um, style of your music is a bit too ... *volatile*, for a school dance."

Volatile? What the freak was that supposed to mean? I didn't know if I had just been insulted or what.

44

"What Mrs. James is trying to say," Alphonse kicked in, "is that we couldn't tolerate anything that loud... or that offensive. It would, after all be a school-sponsored function."

I gripped onto my sticks and felt the drops of sweat forming in my armpits. *School-sponsored function?* I'd like to show him a school-sponsored function.

"What is it *you* are trying to say, Mr. Alphonse?" I asked.

Alphonse sighed. "I really am impressed by your range, as Alex calls it. I just don't think anyone could dance to your music. The beat is all wrong. I just think you might cause too many problems."

In other words, we didn't get the job.

"You don't like us because we're too original," Dariana shot back at him through her microphone. The words echoed in the auditorium.

"We don't need to justify our decision," Mrs. James said softly.

The kids were still in the back of the room. No one had left. Somebody back there in the darkness was giving me a thumbs up. Yo.

We had just been rejected and I was mad. When I felt like that I was used to busting something, but this was school and I was in dangerous territory. I started to bash away on my drums — just some hard, brutal sounds, rolls on the floor tom, heavy pounding on the snare. A couple of kids clapped but Alphonse and James were in the back of the room now shuttling them all away. And then they too were gone. We were alone in the empty auditorium.

45

7

Muzzled

Maybe Alex was afraid they'd kick him off the student council or something. He seemed pretty upset. I guess it would have been a big deal for him to have a chance to play at a dance in front of all his snobby friends. I could never figure the guy out. He had to be involved in anything he thought might make him look good or would give him brownie points.

He wouldn't come out and say anything to Dariana but he put the blame on me. "You blew it, Mick. It was all your fault."

Big freaking deal. We had made our point, didn't we? I figured I could get back at both Alphonse and James by simply doing some damage to their cars in the school parking lot. All my time hanging out with Dave, Lanker and Roach was not a waste. The boys had taught me life skills — tire slashing, stereo removal, gas tank modification and even engine damage. It was just a matter of selecting the right tactic to fit the crime.

I tried to explain this to Dariana. I was sure she'd understand. We'd been muzzled. Our music, her song, would not be heard by the student body.

"Mick, you think in very crude terms."

"Thank you."

"It wasn't a compliment."

"It sounded like one coming from you. You always have such a sweet way of saying things."

"Stop calling me sweet."

"Oh, sorry. I forget that you've been brainwashed by flaky feminists. Babes aren't supposed to be sweet, any more."

"Forget *sweet*. Try *sophisticated*."

"You want to help me roll their cars into the harbour?"

"Grow up. Let me explain sophisticated." And she did.

In truth, the plan she outlined lacked the sting of action that involved serious physical damage but I was willing to go along with anything Dariana wanted out of me. She had me twisted around her finger like a pretzel, as the saying goes.

We knew Alex would never go along with her idea and we decided ahead of time that we'd take the rap for it. We wouldn't let him get punished.

The next morning I met Dariana outside her house and she had the cassette of "The Condom Song" that we'd recorded. We hovered around outside the school until everybody was cosy and comfy in their home rooms. As you might have guessed, it was good old Mr. Student Council

Vice President, the one and only Alex, who had the job of doing the morning PA. He read the announcements and was getting ready to play "Oh Canada."

When the coast was clear, Dariana and I crawled beneath the hallway windows of the office and threw open the door to the school radio station booth. Alex swivelled round as we burst into the room, his finger on the "play" switch.

"What the...?"

But it was our time, not his. I put my hand over his mouth and yanked his chair backwards. He struggled so I had to wrestle him out the chair and yank his arm up behind him.

"Not so rough," Dariana scolded me. But I liked being rough. Despite the fact that we had been playing music together, I never fully trusted Alex. He always thought he was too good and I loved putting turkeys like him in his place.

Dariana looked at the control board. She popped out "Oh Canada" and dropped in "The Condom Song." She cranked up the volume and suddenly every home room in the school was getting a taste of Good Idea Gone Bad.

I let go of Alex and barricaded myself against the door at the onslaught of the secretaries, the principal and Mr. Locksely, the guidance counsellor, but when Gideon, the wrestling coach, showed up, I was overpowered. The door opened. "The Condom Song" was cancelled and we were all in very deep fertilizer.

One verse and one chorus had made it out of the little booth, though, and into the hearts and minds of the kids at our school.

I think I really hurt Alex. Something I did to his shoulder. Not my fault, really. I was used to fighting guys who could fight back, not little boys who get driven around in their momma's Audis.

It was the VP, Mr. Alphonse, who sat us down (with Coach Gideon in the room for back-up, I might add) to read us the riot act. Detention all around. Definite suspension if we tried to stir up any more trouble with the condom machine issue. "It's a dead issue," he said. "You have acted way beyond the bounds of reason. Alex, I'm most disappointed in you for being involved in this escapade."

Alex was rubbing his shoulder. He had every reason to bail out.

"Alex wasn't involved," Dariana said.

"I find it hard to believe that you weren't *all* involved," Alphonse said.

And Alex could have bailed out just then, but he didn't. He said nothing. And for the second time since I'd known him, I think I really liked the guy.

The price you pay for fame. In our case, I think the detentions were worth it. People in the halls were talking about the song. They were talking about GIGB. They were saying it was a *crime* we didn't get the gig playing at the dance. Dariana made up a few more copies of the cassette and started handing them out for kids to listen to. That was still in the days of the "Battle of the Walkman" when teachers were trying to stop kids from listening to headsets on the school grounds. But the Walkman generation was winning. And so was the band. I got a nice little glow walking the halls watching kids mouthing the words to Dariana's song as they went from class to class.

Then one day I was sitting in English trying to get my rest when Mrs. Lyons directed a question at Dariana. We were supposed to be studying *The Mountain and the Valley* by some dude named Buckler. Mrs. Lyons said that the book had been banned in some schools. The class was in the middle of a discussion on censorship, which was never very high up on my list of interesting subjects. Well, after all, this was school.

"Why do you think *The Mountain and the Valley* would be banned from schools?" she asked Dariana.

Dariana didn't like being called on in class, I knew. She had a rep for being a kid who'd lived on the street, who'd been in trouble. Nobody thought she was very smart but I knew better. "I think it's a lot like my song," she said.

Suddenly, everyone in the class was alert. "How do you mean that?" Mrs. Lyons asked.

"Well, I think that people — adults, at least — are afraid of my song because it tells the truth. They feel threatened because they'd rather not have to deal with the difficult issues — things like sex and AIDS."

I was ready for Lyons to shoot her down, tell her that she was changing the subject or something so I jumped to my feet. "We've got a right to express the way we feel about things. Dariana's got a right. We all do. People are going to listen to our song. They're already listening and you can't stop them."

Instead of giving me a hard time, Lyons actually looked pleased. "Good point, Mick. It's good to hear you voicing your opinion in class."

Well, that was a bit of a shock. I sat down, feeling a little dizzy. This was weird beyond belief. I was wondering what was coming over me. Here I was getting involved in some geeked-out classroom discussion and the teacher was actually agreeing with me. Was I losing it or what?

Some other turkey raised his hand and said that just because a song was controversial it didn't mean it was good and that he thought the school made the right decision by keeping out condom machines and by yanking our song off the PA.

I could have wiped up the parking lot with him and his opinions. I was ready to tell him so in front of the class. Who the hell did he think he was to try and keep Dariana's song from being heard?

But then this other freaky thing happened. The Chinese kid who called himself Paul had his hand up. Lyons called on him. I couldn't stand his face and thought it was a big mistake that we had allowed his family into the country, let alone allowing the little slant-eyed creep into the school. Now he was going to throw in his two cents about censorship. He couldn't speak English worth spit.

"Before we left China, my parents got put in jail because of what they said in the newspaper. When they did it a second time, we had to leave the country or they would have gone to prison. Like Mick, I think everyone should be free to speak."

The bell rang. Class was over. I found myself staring at Paul, wondering how it could be that this skinny Asian kid had come to my defense in an argument in English class. It made my skin crawl just to think that we shared something in common at all. And I was beginning to wonder just what the world was coming to.

8

The Crowbar Look

I think that was the beginning of the legend. Even Alex had to admit that the controversy was good, although I do think he never forgave me for being so heavy-handed on him in his little radio studio.

Dariana's old man had given up the idea of ever parking his stupid stationwagon back in his garage because it had become permanent GIGB headquarters. I don't even know why we practised so much or so hard. We just did. The music drove us to it. And every time I turned around, Dariana had a new song she wanted us to try. It seemed like she had a new song for every opinion she had. And the girl had some strong opinions.

Sometimes kids would show up to watch. Like — believe it — we were getting a rep. The Emotional Rangers were a big flop at the dance and somebody tried to sneak a copy of "The Condom Song" onto the sound system, only to get it squelched. This led to some shouts of "Censorship!" but, of course, I wasn't there to see it. You wouldn't catch me at a high school dance when I could be out on the streets having fun.

I have to admit these days I wasn't having as much "fun" as usual as there was a bit of chill between me and my old buds. I guess they were thinking I was a bit of a snot for spending so much time with the band, but this was my life now. They must have been curious, however, once they started to hear about our reputation. And that's why they showed up at Dariana's garage.

We were working on some new material that was really kicking. I looked up from my drums to see ugly old Dave staring back at me. "You're not as good as you used to be," he said. Lanker and Roach just grinned.

I knew what he meant. He meant I was too controlled, not outrageous enough. I guess I had mellowed a little, it was true.

I didn't know what to say to them but they were giving Alex the creeps. Alex said he was going to split early. He didn't say why but the reason was obvious. He went inside to call home for a ride. When his mom pulled in the driveway to collect him, she saw Dave and the boys lounging right there alongside the leaked oil from the Dubinski family car. Alex's mom didn't look too happy to see the quality of our home-grown audience.

Lanker started making crude remarks about Alex's mother and I had to tell them to be polite. Once Alex was packed up and gone, Dave cornered me and said that he was "very disappointed" in how I turned out.

"What is that supposed to mean?" I asked.

He looked at Dariana. "She a feminist?" he asked me. Dave had a problem with any babe who didn't know how to "stay in her place." He lumped them all together as feminists. And he hated feminists more than I ever did. I think he hated them almost as much as he hated fags.

"I don't label myself anything," Dariana told him, not waiting for me to answer.

"Yeah," I said, reinforcing the point.

Roach gave me one of his greaseball laughs. "She's got you whipped, Mick."

What could I say to them? Lanker was leering at Dariana now. They were all trying to get me going so I'd do something stupid. But maybe Dariana had influenced me. I wasn't going to let them get to me.

"We miss you on the street, man," Dave said. "We didn't expect to see you waste your time on this music thing. It's not like your old band. You used to thrash. This is too lame."

"We're good," I said. "You heard what happened at school?"

"It was cute, but we weren't impressed," Lanker said. "If the song had any real impact, it would have made everybody crazy. The whole school would have been trashed."

"Just 'cause kids didn't go wild and destroy the school, you don't think the song meant anything?" Dariana asked.

55

Roach snorted. "Oh, it meant something, all right. It meant that Mick here sold us out."

"What? How did I sell you out?"

"The music, man. The street. The stuff we believe in." Dave was angrier now and shoving a fist at my face.

In their minds I had crossed over a line, turned my back on them. So I was a traitor. There was a rift between us and it was getting wider. What *was* it we had believed in, anyway? We believed in having fun. We believed in cleaning the junk off the streets — the human trash. We believed in making up our own rules.

No. We believed in nothing.

But I hadn't really changed. Not much. I still didn't believe in anything other than what was good for *me*. The only difference was I had decided that the music was good for me. Dariana and the music. I wasn't about to turn my back on those two things to get back in with this pond scum.

"Get out of here," I told Dave. "Go find some little kid to beat up on."

Dave never took my advice well. He hadn't changed. He picked up a crowbar from a corner of the garage and was walking towards me when a car pulled up in the driveway. I guess he figured it was Dariana's old man or something. Or maybe he only wanted to make the threat. If he was gonna thrash me, he'd do it some time when I wasn't ready, some place where nobody but his cronies would see. He'd catch up to me on a dark street and do it. Now he had a chick and maybe her father watching. Dave didn't like wiping out anybody unless he was sure he could get away with it.

I didn't blink. Dave threw the crowbar through the front of my bass drum, ripping the front skin. Then he and the other two split.

It turned out that it wasn't Dariana's father at all but some guy in a beat-up Volvo. As he tried to get out of the car, Dave was walking past and shoved the door back at him angrily, chomping the poor dude's leg.

I studied the damage to the front of my bass drum. No big deal, I said to myself. A lot of drummers play without a front skin on it. Now mine had a big gash in it with a crowbar sticking out. I decided I liked the image. Forget about ticked-off Dave. I'd go with the new look.

The guy who just pulled up seemed pretty confused as he walked towards us. "Friends of yours?" he asked Dariana and me.

"We were just throwing them off the property," Dariana said.

"I thought maybe they were part of the fan club." The guy smiled now and looked around the garage. "You're missing somebody, right?"

"Yah," I said. "What business is it of yours?"

"Oh, sorry," he said, sticking out his hand for me to shake. "I'm Barry Goddard." He handed me a little business card that said, "Barry Goddard, independent producer."

"Am I supposed to be impressed?"

"No, not at all."

"Then what?" Dariana asked him.

"I heard about you guys. A kid from your school let me hear your song, the condom thing. They even have a nickname for you. What was it ... the Rubber Band?"

I groaned. "Spare me."

"Sorry. Look, I liked the tune. I liked the sound. Can I hear more?"

"As you can see, we're missing a guitar. It'd sound pretty empty without Alex."

"Yeah, right. But it's really the songs I'm interested in. Who does the writing?"

I pointed to Dariana.

"You got others?"

"Yeah, lots."

"Play something, okay? Just the two of you. I'll imagine the guitar in my head."

Hey, I didn't care. I'd play music for the Three Stooges if they asked. We did a version of "Downtown Dangerous" and "Me, You and the Other Poor Slob." Dariana's lyrics were getting more edge to them. She was getting more daring and I liked that. My guess though was that we were moving farther out on the fringe. Maybe it was my positive influence. Of course, Alex was getting antsy about the direction. He kept saying we could never "go commercial" with stuff like that. But here we were with some independent producer — very small time, no doubt, but he was interested in us.

"I've got a sixteen-track recording studio in my basement," Barry said when we were done. "I'd like to record all of you some time and see what it sounds like."

Dariana was sceptical. "How much is it gonna cost us?"

"*Nada*," Barry said. "Nothing. I'd just like you guys to see what it sounds like. You're good. Kids are talking."

"What's in it for you?" I asked.

Barry threw his hands up in the air. "Who knows?"

9

Trouble Is My Middle Name

We shouldn't get involved with small-time operators like that," Alex said, as soon as we told him about Barry.

"What could it hurt?" Dariana answered. "We haven't exactly signed any deals. He just offered to record our stuff. At least we might end up with a good demo tape."

"What was he driving?" Alex asked.

"A Volvo," Dariana said, but she didn't tell Alex that it looked like a Volvo that had been driven through the streets of Baghdad during the Gulf War.

"I still think we should polish our material and hold off for a while."

"Let's just do it," I said. I was getting pretty sick of people who had to discuss everything before they acted. "What could it hurt?"

"Kids are asking for tapes of our songs, Alex," Dariana said. "If we could get some good tracks down and do some dubs we could be selling them."

I guess the idea of making a few bucks from our music appealed to Alex. He gave in.

The session was weird but cool. It wasn't exactly a basement studio. Barry *lived* in the basement of an old apartment building. He had a couple of dogs in there that he'd taken off the street. They sniffed me pretty seriously as I walked in. The place was a real dump. You should have caught the look on Alex's face. But after making friends with the dogs (I got down on the floor and sniffed them), I decided I liked this guy.

He did have a sixteen-track recorder but we had to spread out all over his rattly little apartment to get arranged. Dariana ended up in the kitchen with her keyboard. Through the microphone she said, "Barry, why does the only woman here have to get stuck in the kitchen? Isn't this just a little bit sexist?" He got the joke. She had to explain to me later the thing about putting the only woman in the kitchen. So maybe it was funny, I don't know.

Alex ended up in the bedroom with his guitar and both mangy dogs who seemed to thrive on the sound of an electric six-string torqued out on overdrive.

Wouldn't you know it? I had to set up in the bathroom and keep the door closed. "Otherwise, you'll be too loud, Mick. If I want to mix this properly, I need to have you all isolated from each other."

Talk about weird. We were a band trying to play without seeing each other. The headphones helped but it was hard playing without being able to watch Alex or Dariana and I swore it was the last gig I'd ever do in somebody's bathroom.

We recorded "The Condom Song" and "Downtown Dangerous," Dariana's song about her days living on the street. We played it together and then one at a time, listening to the tracks already recorded. I was thinking it was all a waste of time, a big joke, that Barry was just a hack amateur who had been goofing on us.

But then we heard the mix. It sounded *very* good. In fact, it sounded too good. "That's us?" I asked.

"Good Idea Gone Bad just got a little bit better," Barry said.

Barry invested a couple of hundred bucks into dubbing some two-song cassettes and he went around putting them into the record shops. Alex didn't trust him, but that was Alex. We hadn't signed any contracts. Barry was okay. He was going to split anything he made on the cassettes with the band. We kept whatever we made from tapes we sold ourselves to kids in school. For once in my life I had some change in my pocket. I felt like a real businessman.

Then CKDU, the Dalhousie University station started playing "The Condom Song." People all over Halifax and Dartmouth were hearing it. Alex couldn't deny that we were getting attention. It was pretty happening. The music world had changed in a big way from five years ago. It wasn't like the old days when only big time bands made recordings with major labels. Now you could create your own label — like Barry's, called "Magus Music" — and just do it. I could handle the glory. Clearly, if CKDU was giving us airtime, we were cutting edge.

In fact, a guy from CKDU called up Dariana and invited us all in for a live interview. Now, it wasn't exactly MTV or anything but it seemed like a step up. Even Alex was impressed.

So we went down to Dal and we were kind of goofy because we had each dressed up in old raggy duds figuring that we should look very hip and very slashed. Alex had on these John Lennon type shades and Dariana looked … well, just dynamite. I had on a chopped off T-shirt with a picture of Hitler on it. It was short enough to let my gut hang out a little and there were no sleeves so that my armpit hairs stuck out. Some rockers probably take years to achieve this look but for me it comes naturally. I am just lucky that way. Even university kids were looking at us like we must be important as we walked into the Student Union Building. The only thing missing was the stretch limo, but I knew that pretty soon we'd be getting driven around in something better than Barry's old rust hulk.

So we went into the studio and I nearly freaked. There was that fag Stephen working the sound board. He and Dariana hugged and I wanted to gag. Maybe now was my chance to finish the job on his face with my boot.

"You go to school here?" Dariana asked him.

"No, I'm just volunteer at the station," he answered. They were still hugging.

"This is great to see you," Stephen told her. But then the fruit saw me standing there.

What was I gonna do?

I'm sure he had never realized that the drummer of GIGB was the guy who wasted him, the one he described to the cops. He looked at me and I saw fear creep into his face. Then he looked at his watch. Yeah, I was still wearing it. It had brought *me* good luck. But as he was looking at it, I turned my hand into a fist and silently thrust it in the air. I'd kill the little goof if he messed up this scene for us. But I also knew that he had me. If he wanted to call the cops and have me arrested, he could do it.

I tried to get eye contact. I wanted him to know I meant business. *Blab on me, little brother, and you'll soon regret* it. But he looked away. "Time to get you guys on air," he said to Dariana and opened the door to the studio. We walked into a little room that smelled like stale cigarettes and week-old farts.

The interview went okay but I didn't say much. Dariana sounded tough and sharp. Alex came off like the momma's boy that he is and all I got to say was that I learned everything I knew about drumming from listening to old Husker Du and Clash albums. The truth is, I was sweating it because I was there in this little room with no place to run if Stephen wanted to call the law on me. I could feel a dribble of sweat sneak out and trickle down from my arm pit hairs. It made me really angry that a little worthless piece of nothing could get me worried like this.

On the way out, I was relieved to see Stephen was gone. I reckoned my silent threat was enough for a wimp like that to not take chances with getting me in trouble. I was doing okay after all.

Things only got better after that. During lunch at school, a couple of kids started playing our music on a ghetto blaster in the cafeteria. The tape and the box were confiscated. Alex tried to protest this at a student council meeting. He got going on that censorship thing again but nobody else saw it his way. He lost his cool and started yelling at a couple of his other egghead friends. Finally, the student council advisor, Mrs. James, never one of our big-time fans, had Alex booted off student council. And even the local newspaper made a story about it.

Dariana and I thought the publicity for the band was pretty decent. The paper said that "The Condom Song" had "brought back to life the dead issue of installing condom machines in the school washrooms." But some parents were "offended and deeply disturbed by the langauge on the two songs that were being played by students during school hours." Alex was quoted as saying that the music was an expression of "freedom of speech." But Mr. Alphonse had made the case to the press that it was "the music itself that had turned out to be such a bad influence on what was once one of the top students in the school."

It was all just fine with me. I could handle the hassles from any old bat or bean counter who wanted to call us names. Trouble was what I liked. Trouble was my middle name. Dariana didn't seem to mind it, either. She was getting tougher by the minute. "People *do* listen to the words," she insisted.

Meanwhile, Alex had to put up with his mother and father telling him that his fellow band members were flushing his life down the crapper. After getting booted from the council and all the bad publicity, he was having second thoughts.

Dariana and I never saw it coming at all but I guess his parents had really done a number on the guy. He was looking down at the floor when he told us. The words hit us like a hammer to the skull. "I'm thinking of quitting," he told us. "It's costing me too much."

10

Dance Hall Daze

But Alex didn't quit. He knew we had too much going for us. He was still worried about his problems with his mom who was so disappointed in him getting thrown off student council. He missed a couple of practices and by then it was too late for him to make us change our minds about Barry. We were hot and Barry had taken it on himself to be our manager. Dariana and I both liked the guy. We all had this thing in common: we lived for the music. What came out of the recording sessions in the basement was nothing short of a miracle. Also, Barry knew that we were ready for a live audience, so we were flying high when the weird dude announced, "I've got a job for you."

Barry had managed a couple of bar bands before. I figured he must have lied about our ages and got us a booking at a tavern or something. "We get free beer with it?" I asked.

"No. No free beer. Sorry about that, Mick. It's not that sort of gig."

"We'll settle for juice and cookies," Dariana said. "What is it?"

"I rented a hall. We'll promote it on CKDU, put posters up all over town. I think we can pack the joint."

"How much we gonna make?"

"Depends on how many people come through the door. First we pay off the rental, then you guys get all but ten percent. Agreed?"

It sounded okay to me. Shoot, I'd do it for nothing.

"What if nobody shows?" Dariana asked.

"Then I lose my shirt," Barry said, "and you hoodlums get a great place to practice for the night."

The night of the dance, the place was packed, jammed tight with all kinds of people. I'd never been so nervous in all my life. We were set up, ready to blast the place. Barry had even rented a dynamite PA set-up that he was monitoring. It was like big time.

It was a really weird mix of humans — street kids, straight kids from school, Black kids from here in the North End ... and then I spotted my goonie friends, Lanker, Dave and Roach. What the heck were they doing here? Unfortunately, I could guess the answer.

We started off with "The Condom Song" and that got everybody revved up because it was what had established our rep. Then we peeled off into a couple of Dariana's other tunes and I was working away at the drums, feeling like I had just become a superstar. We had all come back together with the music, despite recent differences. That was the way our band was. We fought. We argued. We disagreed. And then when it came down to the music, we worked at it until we were right on the money. Tonight we were like gold.

But, like my old man used to say, "You go flying too high with the birds and you're gonna crash." The night was going too good.

I noticed that Dave had more than just Roach and Lanker along. He had scraped up some other dregs to join him. They were hanging around the back of the hall like the scum line after you drain the bath tub. Our music was loud so we could drown out their insults but between songs, Dave and his boys were shouting some really nasty stuff. It was mostly directed at Dariana — you know, the kind of stuff guys say. Dariana was trying to ignore it but I knew that wasn't her style. She looked at Alex and said the name of the song I was hoping she'd ignore under these circumstances.

Too late. Alex was already launched into the wailing guitar lead of "Downtown Dangerous." I had no choice but to pick up the beat and get into it. "I want to dedicate this one to the boys in the back," Dariana said. Bad news. What ever happened to the old days when women knew when to keep their mouths shut? I tried playing so loud that maybe no one would hear the lyrics but tonight Dariana had the PA and Barry had already cranked up the vocals so even the old Mickster couldn't whack hard enough on his drum kit to drown her out.

Dariana was looking straight at old Davie when she sang the lines:

Problems on the street are the people you meet,
animals, cannibals, racists and creeps,
so stupid and weak they can barely speak
so they beat up on us, they'll pick
anyone
then hide in the dark or they chicken and run.

That was Dariana. Never knew when to keep her opinions to herself. I'd heard the lyrics over and over. I knew where I fit into it but I figured it was only a song. It didn't mean anything. Just a bunch of words. And I liked the way the tune went. I had a great little drum solo near the tail end of it. But now, I guess, this song about the street had gone political.

I looked out into the crowd. Maybe if we could just keep the instrumental part of the song going for like a really long time, maybe seven hours, everybody would just go home. Nothing would happen. I saw more people coming into the room now. Some of Alex's buddies from school — real clean-cut front-row types. I saw some really fine looking babes come in, too. And then, haunting me like a fairy ghost — Stephen. Couldn't the guy take a hint?

The song ended. Alex hadn't been reading the faces. "I'm gonna take a real quick break," he said to me. "I'll be right back."

Before I could say anything, he was off the stage, heading towards the door to meet his friends, Danny and Craig. I guess he was going to have them come up front or something because they had never come to hear us practise. This was a big deal that some of Alex's student council type buds had arrived. But it was mighty bad timing.

Dariana's words had thrown Dave's maniac lever into high gear. He and his buddies saw Alex coming. To Dave, Alex and his friends were a bunch of fruits. That's just the way his mind worked. So Dave figured it was a great time to move in. The goons followed. In a matter of seconds, Alex, Danny and Craig were surrounded by the mob with no brain.

Lanker quickly knocked Danny to the floor and yanked off his jacket. Dave was calling him names. Roach tripped Alex on his face and Craig looked for an exit but one of Lanker's friends shoved him back into this little arena. This was their game and they knew how to play it well. I knew what they were trying to do. They were trying to wreck the dance. Man, I wasn't going to get down there and get involved. Whatever happened, I knew that I'd end up losing so I stayed put.

Barry was trying to get at the centre of things. All the kids had circled around but nobody really knew what was going on. Then I saw Dave about to punch Alex in the face only to have his fist grabbed by Stephen. Oh my god, this was going to be ugly. If it wasn't for the fact that it was ruining the music, I would have loved this scene. I had a great seat up on stage. I could see everything. But tonight was different.

Before Dave could get a good hold on Stephen, Dariana was off the stage like a bolt of lightning and barging into the middle of things. She drove a fist into Dave's crotch and told him to let go of Alex. "Get out of here. All of you!" she shouted.

I think Dave actually felt the punch because he let go of Stephen and stood there staring at her in total disbelief. His cronies were laughing at him now and I knew that we were moving into hurricane season.

Realizing that I had no choice but to get into the middle of things and try to bring calm and reason back into the scene, I reluctantly left my drums and shoved my way into the middle of the arena.

"You touch her," I told Dave, "and I'll hit you so hard your eyeballs are going to squirt out of your ears."

Yeah, it had to come down to me and Dave. I had no choice but I also knew that he had about fifty pounds more than me on his side, that he carried knuckles and maybe a knife, that he really wouldn't lose any sleep if he killed me and that if anything went wrong on his part, he had a very loyal mafia of brainless blobs with him who would settle up the problem by dismembering me in front of the crowd. So I wasn't exactly the happiest lad at the dance.

I knew Barry was screaming at me to not get involved but his path was blocked by part of the Dave team. Craig and Danny were getting up off the floor. Alex was looking for a safe escape route. Dariana was screaming something at Dave that was less than complimentary. And I took the first wallop hard on my left ear. I felt my brain kind of slide from one side to the other, until I could get my balance. Then I planted a big one in Dave's gut knowing that he was very proud of his bloated pot belly and that this was the place to injure his pride.

Dave just smiled and reached out with two hands like a pair of lobster claws and tried to get my head into a vice lock. I tripped him, then tried to tromp on his face only he rolled away and pulled me down, then drove a knee into my back. When I found my way back up onto my feet, I knocked him in the jaw. He got me back and when I felt the first dribble of blood sliding down my chin, I realized that we were both smiling. I hadn't had this kind of fun in a long time.

We were both breathing hard as we heard Lanker yelling at us. He had Stephen in a head lock. "Guys, you're wasting your energy. Stop hassling each other. Look who I got here. Come on. Have some real fun." I looked at Dave and suddenly it was like old times. We felt like brothers. We smiled. I'd forgotten all about the music. Lanker said, "Come on, Mickey, you first. You did it before. You can do it again."

I didn't like that. Now it was out of the can. Dariana was watching me like a hawk. *Okay, okay.* I started towards Lanker. The least I could do was make him let the little fruit go. We didn't need this. But I guess Dariana wasn't so good at reading the look on my face when I had one puffed up eye and a drizzle of blood because suddenly she charged at me and bit hard on my arm. I yelled and nearly wonked her one but caught myself just in time. She really thought I was going to batter her old chum, Stephen.

Well, that's when the cops showed up. They moved towards us through the crowd. Somebody with a megaphone told everyone to leave the building and to get off the property. The dance was over.

I tried to just fade on back toward my drums and pretend I wasn't involved but a pair of the cops had circled round and "wanted to talk" to me as well as to Dave, Lanker, Stephen and Dariana.

One of the policemen recognized Stephen. "You want to tell us what was going on here?" he asked.

I wondered then if Stephen, too, thought I was ready to trash him ... to trash him *again.* He had no reason to believe otherwise, I guess. All he had to do was say the words and I'd be arrested. I realized I was still wearing his stupid watch. He could have nailed Dave and Lanker as well. Typically, Roach had squeezed through some rat hole and made it clear of the hall before the cops got us.

I waited for Stephen to point the finger and for the police to collar me. "It was all a misunderstanding," he said. "That's all it was."

The same cop looked at Dariana. "You wanna explain this."

"It's like he said. It was just a misunderstanding."

I breathed a sigh of relief and rubbed my arm where I felt the indentations left by Dariana's teeth.

11

Getting Groomed

I didn't see what Alex was so upset about. We actually made money on the gig. The cops cleared everybody out so fast that no one had a chance to ask for their money back. Barry paid off the hall and split the take with us. I felt like a rich man with cash in my jeans. I convinced Dariana that it was not my intention to bust Stephen but free him.

"Sorry about the damage," she said, pointing to the purple marks left where she had bitten me.

"No problem," I said. "Besides, I kind of like the way it looks."

Barry had to have a meeting with the cops but they never fined him or anything. And thanks to the ruckus, the rep of GIGB actually increased. Barry had to dub a couple hundred more cassettes. What else could you ask for?

Despite all the good news, Alex was still unhappy. "It's costing me too much," he said again. We were trying to practise in D's garage, trying to get onto a couple more tunes but Alex was getting cranky.

"Costing you? You made money didn't you?"

Alex was sore about him and his buds getting pushed around. It made them look like the wimps that they really were. "We never should have gotten involved with a loser like Mick. It was all his fault. If it wasn't for him and his friends, the dance would have gone without a hitch," Alex told Dariana, as if I wasn't right there.

"I thought you liked the element of danger he added to the band," Dariana said. "Wasn't that the way you put it?"

So there.

"I just didn't know how low we were all going to have to sink. Dariana. Look, we don't need him. It's your songs that matter. We could get another drummer."

What a snotwipe. Alex was still bummed about getting kicked off student council. Then the trouble at the dance. Such a pessimist. He couldn't see that we were hot. Everybody knew it.

I said nothing, for once. Despite the verbal abuse, I was cool. Dariana appreciated that.

"Let's take a break," she said. "I'll get you guys some Pepsis."

"Got any beer?" I asked.

Dariana couldn't see the humour. She gave me one of her death-ray stares. "My father catches you drinking his beer and you'll find a set of tire treads on your face."

I loved it when she talked to me like that. "What a way with words," I told Alex.

Alex just sulked.

When she was out of range I said, "What's with you? I thought you and I had an agreement?"

"I'd never make any deals with you, Mick."

"Without me, this band would be like stale bread."

"Without *me*, this band wouldn't exist," Alex said.

Funny thing, but after we argued like that, we actually played better. Get the grudge going, pump up the heat on ticked-off and suddenly we were cooking.

I started thinking about the fact that some of Dariana's lyrics were about guys like me — well, guys like Dave and Lanker — and I guess I'd have to include myself ... one of the "male pigs who can't do nothin' but grunt." There I was playing the drums on these tunes that were major put-downs on my attitude.

So much stuff in my head to get me confused. *Why didn't Stephen turn me into the cops?* Two chances he had and backed down both times. Weak in the knees or something else?

Late at night, I'd lie in my bed and crank on the radio, tune it in to CKDU, the only station in town that played real music. Man, I couldn't stand that lame pudpucker drivel they played on the other stations. I'd lay there and listen to Cuckledoo (our nickname for the station) until they played one of our tunes. We had six tracks down already, all recorded at Barry's basement studio. I was beginning to feel completely at home sitting on his toilet with my clothes on, playing the drums. But listening to our songs on the radio late at night made me dream about making it big.

I decided I'd beat the brains out of Alex if he kicked me out of the band. He'd have a hard time replacing me. It never occurred to me that he was still thinking of walking out on us. Not with our rep. Dariana was always trying to convince Alex that I was changing. Of course, I wasn't. It was the same old me. All I had learned was to keep my mouth shut and not rant and rave about fags and feminists. The only real reason that I didn't hang out with the Davester and the Roaches was that I just didn't have time, man. I had music. I had a life.

The garage thing was getting to be a real event. You'd never know who would show up. Barry was there sometimes, just listening, every once in while throwing out a little advice, very low key, sort of. Sometimes kids from school would come by and lounge in the driveway. Mrs. Dubinski was getting complaints from the neighbours but she didn't like dealing with them, so she just left her phone off the hook when we played.

Alex mellowed once he started having chicks think he was cool. He had a couple of fans and his grades were slipping. So I figured that maybe he was coming around. But then his old man who owned an advertising business got him in touch with some record scout from a big label — D and D Records. They had signed some really smooth acts like Humble Headbangers, Mind over Matter and Professor Ouija. Big time stuff but all pretty tame music, stuff like you'd hear on C100.

Alex introduced the spiffy dude with the briefcase as Giles Redmond. The man had a handshake like last week's dishwater.

"I've heard your tapes," he said. "I hear potential."

"Cool," I said. "You want to offer us a million bucks?"

Dariana gave me the death-ray.

"Not yet," Giles said, cool as frozen mucous. "I'm just saying we're interested. My job is to work the fringes, find bands like yours and groom them for success."

I didn't like that word "groom."

"Meaning?" Dariana asked.

"Work with you. Fine tune the music, make suggestions as to how to create a more marketable product."

"What's that supposed to mean?" I suddenly felt like I was getting a lecture from some department store stiff.

"Alex and I have been talking," Giles said. "Maybe he can explain."

Alex was all worked up over this guy. They had been hanging out together and I had the feeling that Alex had already made some sort of deal.

"It's like this," Alex began. "Giles is willing to work with us, help us write and produce a few tunes as demos and then make a pitch to the big wigs. This is how it happens. This is the break we've been looking for."

I thought he was going to pee his pants. I wondered what Dariana was thinking but she wasn't showing her cards.

"How much we get paid?" I asked.

"Nothing at first. We invest some time in you. You invest some time in us. If it works out, we all go home happy."

"No money?"

"Not now. But later ..." Hands in the air, fluttering dollars of the imagination.

"We already have a manager," Dariana said. "Barry's been good to us. You heard the tapes. That's his recording work."

"Amateur stuff," Giles said. "If we could get you into a Toronto studio, you'd sound much better."

"When would that be?"

"Depends."

"On what?" she asked.

"On when we get a deal?"

Giles pulled some CDs out of his briefcase. "These are some of our recording artists," he said. "You can keep these."

It was an impressive looking pile of very successful rockers — the Headbangers, Professor O, Mind over Matter, Descreet Destroyers, that sort of thing.

"We've got a deal," Alex said.

Dariana looked worried but said nothing.

I was staring at the CDs and thinking about what it would be like to be as rich as some of those dudes. "Where do I sign?" I asked.

"No contract. Not yet. First we have to see how you respond to our development program."

It sounded like I had just signed up for a body-building course or something but I didn't care. Hey, I was ready for the next big move. I knew we had it coming.

12

Insulting, Obscene and Dangerous

It was at this point a really neat thing happened. We'd sold maybe 500 cassettes and kids all over town were listening to our songs. Our raunchy music and even raunchier lyrics could be heard on any number of headsets all over Halifax and in the far distant parts of Dartmouth. Kids *talked* about the band and about our only live performance that had lasted for four songs. And it was like everybody was waiting for us to do something big.

But we didn't have to do anything at all.

I woke up one Saturday morning feeling lonely and hungry and immediately went over to Dariana's thinking I could bum a decent breakfast. Dariana's father was off playing golf and her mom was sleeping in, so she seemed to enjoy my company. I asked her if she'd mind making me some eggs and maybe a dozen pieces of bacon. I thought she might get into it, you know, having to, like, make me a good breakfast.

"Sure," she said. "No problem." But instead of going right to it like a nice old-fashioned, sensible woman, she took a whole pack of raw bacon out of the fridge, slipped it out of the wrapper and said, "Hold out your hands."

I was thinking she was going to hand me a plate but instead she handed me this big greasy wad of bacon.

"You like it raw, don't you?" she said. "You said you wanted eggs, too?"

"No thanks," I said, putting the bacon back in its wrapper and wiping my hands off on the tablecloth. "I'll just make myself some toast."

That's when Dariana opened up the *Chronicle-Herald* and discovered our good fortune. A story on page eight said that a bunch of parents had declared our music to be "insulting, obscene and dangerous." Three sweeter words had never found their way into the English language. These good-hearted, upstanding adults called themselves Parents for Musical Morality.

According to some lady named Mary Montgomery, "The Condom Song" showed a "serious lack of respect for authority and promoted promiscuity in teenagers." Mrs. Montgomery had heard her fourteen-year-old daughter playing our beloved tune on the living-room stereo instead of listening to the family collection of elevator music. And Mrs. Morality Montgomery proceeded to go through the roof. She found an ally in the form of Richard Garber, another parent whose son had been warped out of his morality by our music and was forever damaged because he had listened to the lyrics of "Downtown Dangerous."

"It's censorship again," Dariana said. "They can't do this."

"Of course they can," I said, spraying fragments of toast around the room as I talked. "If people like to hate our music, it means we must be doing something right."

"How come the paper didn't ask us to comment?"

"Dariana, don't get so serious about this. It's just a bunch of old geeks with hormonal deficiency trying to stop us from having fun."

"Yeah, but they're also trying to censor us."

"Let 'em. Kids love anything their parents say is bad for them."

"Yeah, but the Parents for Musical Morality are going to be picketing those record stores that carry our tapes. And they're going to try to have CKDU's broadcasting license revoked."

"I'll bust their legs," I said.

Dariana never knew when I was joking. But then neither did I.

"You always revert to primitive notions of masculine aggression when you're upset, don't you?"

"What's wrong with that?"

"Nothing a good brain transplant wouldn't cure," she said. The way she said it really ticked me off. I was getting tired of Dariana putting me down all the time. She still couldn't accept me for who I was, and that really bugged me. When would she give it up and stop trying to turn me into something I wasn't?

While I was sulking, Barry called to say he'd read the story and already talked to a couple of the independent music stores. Nobody was ready to back down and pull our music from the racks.

We hadn't said much to Barry since Giles had shown up, but now that he had called us, I guess Dariana felt it was time to give him the low-down. "Come on over to our practice session this afternoon," Dariana told him. "There's somebody I think you should meet."

That somebody was Giles. I knew this was going to be awkward but Dariana figured that together, Barry and Giles could help us plan a counter-attack on the PFMM.

When we were setting up, Alex said that his mom had friends who were joining this musical morality thing.

"Alex, it doesn't mean you have to worry about it. She's only your mother," I said.

"You don't know how much flack I put up with to stay in this band."

"My heart is bleeding big puddles of blood for you, Alex. But grow out of it. What your mom's friends think doesn't mean squat. They're all gonna be dead in forty years and we're all going to still be hammering music."

Barry was already there. He was running full support mode. "Yeah, man. Don't let it get to you. They start censoring your songs and who knows where it will end? When I was a kid they tried to stop us from reading *One Flew Over the Cuckoo's Nest* in school and they tried to pull Hendrix songs off the air because they thought they were about drugs."

"They were about drugs," Dariana reminded him.

"Well, the point is, you can't stop writers and musicians from being creative by putting limits on what they are allowed to say. It's freedom of speech."

I was afraid this was going to get real boring. Already the dude had mentioned the title of a book and I didn't read books. I was afraid he'd get all wired up in one of his sixties raps and we'd have to listen to it. So I made a musical comment by doing a heavy roll on the snare drum. Barry took the hint, looking a little hurt.

"Just trying to loosen up my wrists, man. Sorry."

"You don't need to apologize," Barry said.

"I'm going to write a song directed right at these self-righteous music-haters," Dariana asserted.

"I don't know," Alex said. "I just don't know. It doesn't feel right."

I didn't get what he was talking about. Of course it felt right. A song that trashed a bunch of lame prudes was an excellent idea. I knew Dariana would make it good and angry which would give me a chance to come up with a really pounding beat.

And then there was Giles. Giles didn't take off his shades when he came inside the garage. Giles wore shoes that probably cost more than my whole drum set. He had a snotty way of hanging out that told me he thought he was really very important.

Barry sized him up like a mortal enemy. He introduced himself.

"I've heard about your work with the band," Giles told Barry. "You've done good. D and D respects guys like you who help out with the first step in a career."

"Right."

"The band has told you about my interest?"

"Yeah," Barry said. "We've been working together. I've been acting as a manager but we don't have any formal arrangements. I believe in these guys. Whatever they want for their career is okay by me."

That was typical Barry. Never pushy. Always very sixties about everything. I knew that the Gilesman here was horning in on the territory that Barry had carved out for himself. Old Bar had invested his time and moola in us and we were ready to leave him in the dust for D and D. But the dude didn't seem to mind. Maybe he was just a born wimp.

"Have you seen this?" Barry asked. He handed Giles a copy of the *Herald*.

Giles dipped his glasses. He read the words slowly, moving his lips, just like me when I read.

Alex tried to get his guitar in tune to Dariana's keyboard but he was having a hard time of it. I knew something was bothering him. I was getting really tired of sitting there doing nothing. "Let's do some music," I said.

"I'm not in tune," Alex snapped.

"So what?"

"Can you give us a minute, Mick?" Dariana interjected.

I took a break and walked outside. I was tired of being polite. I figured that our fame now rested on the fact that we were considered insulting, obscene and dangerous, and we should start living up to that image. Who would care if we were in tune?

Barry borrowed Alex's guitar to help him get it locked in tune. That's when Giles sidled over to me outside on the driveway.

"This thing in the paper is not so good for you," he said, all confidential now, like he was telling me some hot new secret.

I almost laughed. "It isn't?" I asked.

"The company will not look favourably on bad publicity. Not at this stage of your career, anyway."

"Why not?"

"Because you're going to alienate that whole audience who would listen to you on commercial stations."

"But I thought a bad rep was good."

He shook his head. "A bad rep is good if you've already established a good rep as being *bad*, in the musical sense, before you cross over to being bad in the real world, where maybe you break a law or something."

It sounded like double-talk to me. "No kidding?"

"No kidding. Look, Mick, I can tell you're a reasonable guy with a level head."

He had me pegged right down to the wire.

"That's why I'm going to ask you to help me with this one. Persuade Dariana that Good Idea Gone Bad needs some material that is more commercial, something that won't offend anyone. Just plain music. You have good musical abilities. You three carve a weird and intriguing image. All you need is the right material. Don't let the language turn off a huge chunk of your potential audience."

"You're messing with my head," I told him.

"Listen. Let's be straight. What do you want ... out of your career? You wanna be recording in basements and selling cassettes to your friends at school or you wanna record in the best studios in North America and make megabucks?"

"I'd say the megabuck thing sounds like a good choice."

"Good," said Giles. "Now we're speaking the same language. Alex is already with me on this one. But I thought you could help me with Dariana. You know how she is."

"It's from hanging around with too many feminists," I said. "Sure, I'll try to sweet talk her on this one."

I didn't really know what I was agreeing to. I mean the guy had a good point — about the money and stuff. I still didn't care about the words in the songs. I had my eye on the end of the rainbow and I didn't want to get off course.

Alex and Dariana were in tune. Barry was sitting on some boxes in the corner.

"I'm gonna be sending up a sample of your work soon to T.O.," Giles said to Dariana. "I think we have a fair sampling of your rough stuff but I'd like you to come up with a couple of tunes that aren't quite so far off the centre?"

"What's that supposed to mean?" Dariana asked.

"You know. Something more commercial, more pop. They'll want to hear a balance of songs. They'll want to know if you're a one-hit wonder or a versatile band that can be groomed."

There was that dog word again. Yuck.

"I had a couple of ideas I've been working on," Alex jumped in. "Listen to these chord riffs."

Alex whipped off some basic chord structures and suggested a rhythm to me. It was kind of light, kind of air-head danceable but I found myself going along for the ride. Giles was smiling now. Alex was smiling. Barry and Dariana were looking at us like we had just transformed into the Lunenburg Polka Band. I knew exactly what had happened just then. Alex and Giles had come up with a little plan. I had just joined the conspiracy and we were heading one step closer to the middle of the road.

Giles had his glasses off. He winked at me now. I felt like I had just let the Prunepits for Morality have a cause to celebrate. But, hey, it was just a temporary compromise. And I was willing to go for it if it meant getting a contract with D and D. It wasn't like selling out or anything. It was just learning the ropes.

Dariana hammered on a whole pile of keys at once. "What is this putrid slop?" she screeched.

"It was sounding good," Giles said.

"Come on, Dariana," Alex complained. *"Yo*u always initiate all the songs. I'd like some input for once. Let's roll with this. You and I can write the lyrics. We can work on it."

"I don't like it," she said. "It's not us."

"We have to learn to grow — creatively, I mean," Alex said.

"This isn't growing. This is something else."

"I say we do a few more commercial tunes that Giles can take with the other stuff to T.O.," Alex said, now sounding like he was back in the middle of a student council meeting.

"And I say we don't back down for anybody but we stick to our style of music."

"Okay," Alex said. "Let's take a vote."

It was democracy in action. Only problem was there were three of us. Alex was on one side of the barbed wire fence, Dariana was on the other and my butt was squarely on the ragged metal edge of the top wire.

"I'm with Alex," I said. Sure, I felt like a traitor — big time. But I figured it would be worth it in the long run.

So Giles paid Barry to record us again in his basement — two new tunes that Alex wrote, with some coaching from Giles. Dariana wrote the lyrics but Giles took an axe to them and changed them around so that they sounded like a lot of that drippy nonsense on C100. Dariana wasn't pleased but she went along with it grudgingly. Giles made the promise that if we could get our foot in the door, then we could go back to doing anything we wanted to. The only difference was that we'd be getting some real gigs, we'd be making some real money and we'd be on the road to rock music heaven.

The tunes were bland, the music so-so, the drumming like something out of a can but Giles loved it and sent the noise off to Toronto.

Meanwhile Giles had met with the PFMM and told them about our new direction. He told us it was "damage control" but he wouldn't tell us exactly what he had said to them. The Morality Squad never did protest outside the record stores but suddenly CKDU was playing a lot less of our two big hits.

13

A Night in the Cemetery

Giles wanted to celebrate. He made it sound like we were headed for big time. I thought we'd have like a real wild party or something but instead, he took us out to a restaurant called the New World. They didn't have anything but goopy foreign food. Nothing real — no pizza, no burgers or fried chicken. Dariana thought it was cool but I thought it sucked. It was very boring, let me tell you. I bowed out at about nine o'clock, thinking I could at least get out into the night, maybe run into some action. Anything to get away from wonky food and tea that smelled like perfume.

I knew that if we made it big, we'd get to play major gigs then we'd trash hotel rooms and neat stuff like that. If Dariana and Alex weren't into it, then I'd have to rely on my fan club to help me out. This was the sort of thing going on in my head as I headed downtown. Despite the boring meal, I was thinking about my glorious career — what I'd wear on stage, how the girls would re-act, whether or not to get a tattoo of a snake on my forehead. That sort of thing.

Nothing was happening in front of the library. I guess Dave and the boys had found a new haunt. A couple of cops in a squad car were shovelling donuts there on the street, in the spot where Bud the Spud usually parks in the daytime.

I thought I'd just cruise on down through the old cemetery before I headed home. It was dark and spooky, surrounded by tall trees. After sitting in a boring restaurant, I needed something with a taste of weirdness and danger. I opened the gate and walked the path leading past a huge dark statue, past the lines of tombstones. I couldn't hear anything at first except gravel crunching under my feet, but then there was a noise — a scream.

I stopped. There was the sound of someone getting hit — hit hard. I heard him groan from the pain. I heard somebody else laugh. The laugh told the whole story. I'd recognize the sound of Roach getting his fun anywhere.

Slowly I walked closer, staying behind some bushes so I wouldn't be seen. Why didn't I just go right up to them and join in? I'd played this scene before. What was holding me back?

Now it was all different. I wasn't a part of it. I was what you'd call an innocent (or not-so-innocent) bystander. I didn't know who was being trashed. Could have been some gay creep. They were known to hang out in this place sometimes. They were also known to get beat up here. Dave, Lanker and Roach had always talked about how much fun it would be to do an honest-to-god stake-out. I reckon tonight was their night.

Keeping my distance, I stayed behind some bushes and shifted around so that I could get a good view of what was happening. There was only a little street light getting through the branches but I got the picture clear enough. A guy was down, curled up like a baby now. The only sound he made was from the air coming out of his mouth in short bursts when Lanker kicked him in the gut. I heard Dave talking to the guy, telling him he deserved what he got, telling him that this was some sort of lesson.

What happened in my head just then is pretty hard to explain. Maybe I'd been hanging out with Dariana too much, listening to the lyrics of her songs. I wanted to just turn around and get out of there. I didn't want any part of this scene. The words of "Downtown Dangerous" were jammed inside my head, haunting me more than any cemetery ghost could.

I felt confused and a little crazy. Then I edged further left and got a good look at the maniacal smile on Roach's face. I watched as he kicked the guy in the chest as hard as he could, backed off, turned around and did it again. He did it as if in some kind of a dance. He did it to entertain Lanker and Dave. This wasn't like the beating we gave Stephen in front of the public library. There was no one else around here. I had no idea how long this had been going on. And it was just like

Roach to keep a thing like this going until ... until when?

Dave and Lanker had probably already grounded the guy, already punched his lights and knocked the wind out of him. Roach's idea of fun was to finish somebody off, but before, we'd always been interrupted. We'd always had to split before we got caught.

That wasn't going to happen here, I suddenly realized. I saw Dave now reach down and punch the guy in the head. They weren't going to quit. Maybe they were going to kill this guy.

I felt sick to my stomach. I wanted to just run away from there real bad. I didn't want to be around to see it. I didn't want to get involved. The ugly thing in my head was that I knew that I'd been part of this scene. But what about now? *Run*, said the voice inside me. *Just get the hell out of here and don't tell anyone what you saw. It's not your responsibility.*

But my feet didn't want to run. Instead, I made some noise. I scuffed my shoes in the gravel. I cleared my throat. I rustled the bushes. No way was I going to show myself but I was counting on the fact that my old buddies hadn't changed. They loved to get their fun, but they sure as heck didn't want to get collared for it.

Would they come after me or would they just high-tail it?

"Who's there?" Roach asked.

I didn't say anything. That would be best. I was breathing hard. Let them think someone was watching but don't let them know if it's one person or two. Above all, don't let them know it's me.

Lanker walked in my direction but he couldn't see me. What little light there was came from behind me. I could see him, though. And I could see that he was scared now. Scared that he'd get caught in the act.

He didn't say anything. He turned. "Let's get out of here," he told Dave.

The three of them ran off towards the cemetery gate. They were running hard and they were running fast. Sometimes we'd just take our time and kind of jog away from the scene of the crime but this was different. I knew what that meant. If they were this scared, it was because they had done some real damage. The price would be high if they were caught and that's why they were running fast, running scared from anyone who might confront them, anyone who could pin the blame.

They were gone. I was still standing behind the bushes, maybe twenty feet from where this guy was curled up on the ground. Now what? Hadn't I done my bit? Why wasn't I getting out of there, too?

It was crazy but I had to see how bad off this guy was. I slowly walked towards him. "You all right?" was all I could say.

There was no answer. I hunched down and got a look. Blood on the face. Arms still gripped around his gut. "You okay, man?" I asked. Stupid question. Again no answer. He was unconscious.

I leaned over. I think he was breathing but it was too hard to tell because I was panting and my heart was pounding away. A new fear gripped me. *If anyone found me here now, I'd get blamed for this*. It would be easy to pin the blame on me. *Run*, that voice inside me said.

But I also knew that if I left him here like this, he might not be found. I was sure that if he didn't get help right away, this guy — whatever he was, straight, gay, stupid immigrant or whatever — was going to die, and I wasn't about to let that happen.

"I'll get help," I said to him, even though I knew he couldn't hear.

Man, I never felt more scared or more responsible for someone else's life! I tripped twice as I tried to make it back to the street. I thought of running up to the cops on Spring Garden Road, hoping they'd still be parked there, but it was too far away, maybe too dangerous for me. The near-lifeless image of that guy back there kept jumping up inside my head.

I found a phone, got an operator and had her put me through to the police.

I told the man who answered about the scene in the cemetery. I told him exactly where to go.

"He needs help bad. Send an ambulance. Do it quick, man. I'm serious."

The voice on the other end was cool as ice. "I got it. Stay on the line." I heard him fire off the location over the radio to a cruiser and then he was back on the line.

"Okay," he said to me. "We've got somebody on the way. You want to tell me your name?"

I held onto the phone for a second and looked at it. Then I slammed down the receiver. No way were they going to get my name.

But it still wasn't over for me. I was afraid they might not find him. It was a dark night and it was a big cemetery. So I ran back to the beat-up guy. He was still on the ground, not moving. "It's okay," I found myself telling him. "I got help."

I stayed there with him. I didn't do anything but I stayed there until I heard footsteps hurrying towards us. Then I sneaked back into the bushes and ducked down low. First, there were two cops. They checked him over. One guy started giving mouth-to-mouth. Then two other men arrived with a stretcher. When the guy was carried away, the cops stayed behind and shone their flashlights in all directions. I had to stay low and quiet but when they moved away a few more feet to pick up something on the ground, I turned and ran like crazy.

They heard me. "Stop!" one of them yelled, but I never turned around. I ran again into the night. I wasn't going to be around to talk to any cops. I ran just like I had done before. Only now something was different. I was still scared, I was still running but it felt more like I was running away from myself than from the cops.

14

A Dangerous Game

I kept a low profile over the weekend. I didn't show up for practice on Saturday. I sat in my room and listened to metal music or watched the tube. My mother kept asking me to do stuff around the house, but I told her to get lost. My old man kept trying to give me lectures about not being so nasty to my mother, but I told him to leave me alone.

"If you don't want to do what your mother tells you," my old man confided, "don't say you won't do it. Just say you're busy and you'll get around to it later. Maybe she'll forget she asked you and everybody will be happy. I know I shouldn't tell you this, but it's how your mother and I get along. You've got to learn how to handle women, son."

Great advice from my old man. I said I'd try to stick by it.

The business about the guy getting beat up was a pretty big deal. It was all over the news. He nearly died. The TV newsman referred to me as "the unidentified caller, a young male who saved the man's life."

Maybe I should have felt like a hero. But I didn't. Not by a long shot. I was full of really mixed up feelings, full of a kind of anger — anger at my old gang, mainly, but also anger at me. Why exactly was I mad at myself over this?

When I put my fist through the wallboard in my room, my mother was pretty upset. She said I did it because television was such a bad influence.

"Tell your mother you're sorry and that you'll fix it," my father said.

"I'm sorry," I said. "I'll fix it later, okay?"

I went out for a walk and found myself stopping in front of a newspaper box. The headlines in the *Daily News* read, "Gaybashers Strike in City Cemetery." They had a word for it now: *gaybashing*. I bought a paper and sat down to read the story. The victim had recovered enough to give an interview to the papers and said that he was gay and that's why he had been attacked by "young thugs." The police talked about "teenage violence" and "street gangs." They had statistics about the increase in fights and about people being attacked, but it all seemed to be missing something. There was one question screaming at me: *Why were we doing these things?* I knew all about exactly *how* it happened. I knew how I felt. I knew what Dave, Lanker and Roach must have been thinking the other night. But I didn't know *why* we felt that way. Up until now I had never cared. We liked being angry, and it felt good to trash something or someone.

The TV and the newspaper people didn't understand anything about this. I kicked hard at the glass in the newspaper box. It was plastic. It didn't break, which made me even angrier, so I kicked it over and stomped on it hard until the side was nicely dented in. Feeling only slightly better, I went back home, back to my room. No more newspapers, no more TV. All I had in my room in the way of drums was one old snare drum. I started playing and didn't quit until it was dark and my parents had left the house to get some peace and quiet.

On Sunday, in Dariana's garage, she gave me hell for missing practice on Saturday, but she said that it wasn't all a waste. She'd conned Alex into working on a new tune — something like their old stuff. Alex had gone along to make her happy.

Giles wasn't around to groom them. He'd flown to Toronto to push their demo to the bigwigs at D and D. So Dariana had reverted to her old ways. She'd written a really hard, pounding tune with some angry lyrics, some four-letter words. It took me no time at all to come up with the right percussion to fit. I couldn't really hear the words but I knew I liked the song.

On the fifth try, we got it tight. When the wailing guitar lead and the crashing cymbal began to fade at the end, I discovered we had an audience. Barry.

"Giles is going to hate it," he said. He was smiling.

"It's only one song," Dariana said. "If he doesn't like it, it's his problem. We can do other stuff, too. He doesn't have to approve of everything we do."

"But I thought you'd already gone commercial. I thought you left this original stuff behind."

"No way," Dariana said.

"Well," Alex corrected. "We have to try new material. Dariana came up with this. It was important to her, so we worked on it. Gotta keep everyone happy, right?"

"Right," Barry said. "Can we record it tonight? While it's still fresh?"

"Yes," Dariana said instantly. I sensed conspiracy here.

"Maybe we shouldn't," Alex objected.

"I say we do it," I said immediately. It was two out of three again. I felt bad about having pushed Barry off to the sidelines and letting Giles have so much say. We couldn't do wimp-out music all the time.

It wasn't until I got out from behind the drums in Barry's bathroom and got a listen to the first mix that I realized what the song was about. It was about gaybashers. It was about the incident in the cemetery. Dariana had told the story almost like she'd been there, like she'd seen it happen. She was good and mad about it, angrier than I'd ever heard her.

Dariana was smiling and looking straight at me as the tape stopped on Barry's recorder.

"Now *that* is a song," Barry said.

"It's too controversial," Alex insisted. "I don't want the tape to go beyond this. It's going to turn people against us again. Look at the language. It's gonna make those Morality Moms unhappy. And what about the creeps who do the stuff you're talking about, Dariana? They're going to be offended and come looking for us." Alex sounded like a real noodle now. "Besides, Giles would hate this."

"We've already established that Giles would hate it," Dariana snapped. "So what?"

"So we have our careers to think about."

I wasn't getting involved in the conflict but I knew what it was coming down to. One said yes, one said no.

"Alex is right, " I said. "It could be bad for our careers." But I wasn't really thinking about careers. I was thinking about the issue. I didn't want to get involved in it. It was all too close to home.

Dariana walked over to me now. She grabbed the drum sticks out of my hand and glared.

"What is this, a threat?" I asked.

She took the sticks and tapped out something like a code on the watch on my wrist.

"Take it any way you want," she said.

"It's okay," Barry said, sounding really disappointed. "We can just save it in the can. When you hit the big time, I can just listen to it for my own private enjoyment and realize what might have been."

I was looking for a way out of this. I pretended that it wasn't Dariana but Barry who had just changed my mind. "Ah, what the heck. We put all this time into it. Let's send out a few dubs around town. Maybe see if Cuckledoo radio wants to play it. What can it hurt?"

"No, dammit," Alex said. "Absolutely not. Dariana, you lied to me. You said that if we worked this one up, if I went along, just for you, you'd have it out of your system so we could work on some more commercial tunes. There's no way I'm going to let any of you release this."

But nothing Alex said stopped us. It went to Stephen at CKDU and he persuaded the guys there to play "Back off, Bashers!" every hour for forty-eight hours straight. It grabbed hold of the attention of enough kids in town to make it the talk of the street and the talk of the school.

What's weird is that you'd think that because it was a song putting down gaybashers and violence, a lot of adults would have liked it. But that wasn't the case. Some very strict religious parents caught their kids with copies of the song and blew the whistle on us, calling us "obscene (again), insulting (again), and (of course) dangerous to the minds of youth." The Parents For Musical Morality resurfaced, and actually picketed CKDU and the downtown record shops that sold our home-grown tapes.

There were editorials against *us* now in the papers and, in some bizarre way, people were linking the anger in Dariana's song — the anger *against* violence — with the violence itself. PFMM wanted the press to believe that our music was somehow responsible. We were, as they claimed, dangerous. Our music should be banned — in schools, on the radio and in record stores.

Alex was angry alright, but not about the same things as Dariana. If anybody asked me, I didn't say anything about the tune but, "Hey man, it's only a song. It doesn't mean nothin'." I liked playing it stupid. It was an easy way out and it allowed me to roll with all the punches. None of the people who were complaining got to me, though.

Well, that's not quite true. One of the critics did. Dave. Dave called me up late one night to say, "Mick, I know exactly what you've become now. You're a bloody traitor. We want you to know that we hate your song, man. We think you've been brainwashed. We feel sorry for you, brud. We think you should be careful, you know. Real careful."

There was nothing to say so I just hung up. Because of our song, I was somehow connected with what had happened in the cemetery that night. Once again I thought about how I'd crossed the line. The Mick I once was no longer existed. I was this other person. Here I was, late at night standing in the darkness of my house, wondering who I was, what was going to happen next in this crazy mess, and just how dangerous this whole game had become.

15

An Empty, Unhappy Guy

You blew it," Giles said when he walked into the garage.

"Giles, we came up with a piece of music that means something to people," said Dariana in defense of our action. "We said what no one else in this city was willing to say — the truth."

There was this spooked look on Alex's face. I knew just what he was thinking. I was thinking it too — career down the tubes. All because we tried to humour a babe. Or was it more than that?

"Giles, it was a mistake."

"Well, D and D can't afford those kind of mistakes. You know, I'm really disappointed that you guys didn't consult with me first on this one. There I was up in T.O. making the pitch for Good Idea Gone Bad. I played those new tracks you did. They agreed you had started out rough but were moving in the right direction. But now this."

Giles held his sunglasses in his hand and looked out the driveway. There were some kids cruising by on skateboards — little punk kids like the ones that used to make me sick. When they saw us set up in the garage, one kid in a loud yellow shirt yelled out, "Back Off Bashers — good tune. Way to go, dudes." His buddies howled in a kind of hound-dog sound that meant they liked the song as well.

I smiled, but Giles didn't see the point. He picked up a rock and chucked it in their direction. It skidded down the driveway and caught the wheels of one of the skateboards, then bounced into the side of his Trans Am parked at the curb. I nearly broke out laughing.

Giles tried to get control of himself. He rubbed his forehead, put his shades back on and said, "I'm thinking of cutting my losses and running."

"You can't do that," said Alex the Wimp. "We made one lousy little mistake."

"One *big* mistake," Giles corrected. "D and D doesn't want this kind of bad publicity. Especially not from a green band — one that doesn't even have a contract."

Screw the contract, I was ready to say. I didn't know if I could put up with any more of this creep's lecture. Fame, fortune and wrecking hotel rooms suddenly seemed like a fading dream.

"But I've already invested a lot of time in you guys. You know what my time is worth on an hourly basis?"

No one ventured at a figure. My guess was that his time was worth bean squat, but he obviously thought he was one hot recording scout.

"Maybe we can do damage control again," he continued, pacing about the garage. "D and D can donate some money to that campus radio station and request they pull the tune. I'll talk to the record stores myself. If we can nip this thing right here in Halifax, it won't go any further. No more sale of dub tapes, no more airplay and maybe we can calm down the morality people."

"So it's back to censorship," Dariana said, her arms crossed in front of her.

Giles pointed a finger at her now. "Look, do you want to throw it all away? You want to stay a garage band forever? How much money are you making now? How many gigs have you lined up? You think that small-time, over-the-hill hippie, Barry, is going to do you guys any good?" Giles was all revved up now. "Barry doesn't know anything about the music business. I do. I know how things work. I know two things. I know what it takes to make it in this business and I know you guys have what it takes. But I'm going to need you to commit yourself to my game plan, go along with my decisions."

He put his glasses back on. That was cool because it looked as if his eyeballs were about to pop out of his skull like those cartoon characters in Roger Rabbit.

"Giles is right on," Alex said. "Look, he's giving us another shot. Let's take it."

"Censorship and all?" Dariana asked Alex, but staring at Giles.

"It's compromise, that's all," Alex said. "It's business."

I was thinking, *Oh no. Here we go again. Democracy in action.* Man, my head was messed up. I was still thinking about the poor guy who got beat up. I was thinking about me getting involved. I had already taken a stand for something. What, I don't know. But now there was this other stuff. If I said the wrong thing here, I was maybe going to lose the music, lose another band and my only shot at making it big.

Dariana was looking at me and she looked uncertain, worried. "I don't know if I can do it."

What did she want out of me? Why was she looking at me? "Sure," I said, trying to reassure her. "You can do it. We all can."

That was the way it was. She wanted *me* to say it was okay to go along with Giles. I mean, the guy was really putting the screws to us. If he walked now, then, like he said, it would be a big waste. No more chance at the big time.

"I've gotta have an answer. I've gotta hear it from all of you. I need a hundred percent or I'm out of here. No more games."

Games. The word stuck in my head. That's what my life had been up to now. Games. Always games. Teasing people, beating up on them. Hanging out with Dave and the gripe squad. Was it time to get serious? Time to grow up? Or was it one more stupid game?

I looked at Giles. He was staring at me from behind his hundred-dollar sunglasses. The lyrics to Dariana's song went through my head and seeing my image in the mirrors of Giles shades — what I saw at first was me sitting at my drums. But no. Then I saw me crouching over the beat-up slob in the cemetery.

I was supposed to say something now, supposed to say I was in, that I was *serious*, willing to go along for the ride.

"I can't do it, Giles. And neither can Dariana."

Dariana looked stunned. "What are you doing? You can't answer for me."

"Sorry, babe."

But Dariana didn't have to say anything more.

"I don't freaking believe this!" Giles screamed.

"Believe it," I said.

"Mick, you're out of your mind!" Alex shouted at me.

"I'm sorry about the hundred percent stuff, Giles. I really am. But I've never been very good at going along with the crowd. Besides I'm too lazy to make a career out of anything. I just like to bash, man. I didn't want to get *serious*. I didn't know about all this business bull. I guess I just can't hack it. Sorry, brother."

Alex looked like he was having a hard time breathing. I'd slid into a little trip that felt right. I *knew* what it was all about, but I didn't have to come out and say it. I knew where Dariana had been coming from all along. And now I wasn't about to let her back down. What I was really saying didn't have to be said.

"Mick is right," Dariana said now, smiling at me — for the first time looking like she really had a thing for me. "I think I'm lazy too. Career sounds too much like work. I think we'll just keep doing what we're doing."

And that was the end of Giles. That was the end of Alex, too, and there went our shot at a million dollars and a chance to trash hotel rooms across North America.

I can't say I blame Alex. He knew what he wanted and he didn't give up. Within a week he got together with a couple of older guys from a band called Prime Target that had just broken up. They redid those two commercial tunes that Alex and Dariana had worked on. Giles got interested, trying to pick up some of the scrap metal left over from his time "invested" in GIGB. Maybe Alex would still get what he wanted.

That left Dariana and me. Since my little speech, we had become good "friends." I wanted more than that. She knew it. All she could say was, "Mick, I didn't think I'd ever hear myself say it, but I respect you now."

Respect was not what I was interested in. Big deal.

We spent a lot of time together. Still doing music, still practising. In the mind of our faithful local audience, Good Idea Gone Bad still existed. Our songs were still getting airplay, our dubs still selling downtown. But a band without a guitar is like a horse without legs. Very lame.

Dariana and I worked up a tune called "Sell-Out," about Giles and about D and D and how we saw the commercial record industry. Boy, we were good at alienating people. We figured that if we had already cut some ice by being a controversial band then we needed to keep up our image.

Barry lined up a buddy of his, Warren, to sit in for guitar and work on the tune but I could tell from what I heard, sitting in the bathroom with my drums, that it was pretty weak. The lyrics were good, the song was decent and Barry thought the tracks reminded him of the "early days of the Rolling Stones," but it was wimped out. Without Alex's wild, wailing guitar leads, we just weren't a band. Warren was used to playing jazz, not real music, so I didn't hold it against him.

The tune got some CKDU airplay. Hey, they would have played a track of me blowing my nose at that point. Those guys still thought we were hot. But we definitely were not.

About this time, everything began to fade. People were starting to lose interest in the gaybashing problem. I think all the hoods in the city were keeping cool for a while with all the legal eyes out to nail them.

We tried a few guitar players but we were all too far apart. Our old rep attracted some guys with no talent and large egos and we always said thanks but no thanks. Despite the fact that our music was still out there, the band had ceased to exist. As our music faded, so did my so-called relationship with Dariana. I took her out to the movies once but she wouldn't let me do anything more than put my arm around her.

"Mick, I still think we're just too far apart in our thinking."

"How can you say that, babe?" I asked her outside the theatre beneath the glow of a solitary streetlight.

"Takes a long time to change an attitude."

Things went a little arctic after that. I walked her home, she pecked me on the cheek with a kiss that said zero and then I went walking again.

I felt hurt, what can I say?

No babe, no band, no buds. I think I felt like I had just been trapped. I was alone and it felt rotten. I was nobody — an empty, unhappy guy walking around the city at night.

Dave, Lanker and Roach were nowhere to be found. I tried the library, I tried the cemetery, I tried some other hang-outs but the boys must have been lying low. Maybe I was ready to beg forgiveness and hope they'd ask me back. Maybe I was tired of being off the street and I missed the action. If Dave wanted to try and smash my face, just let him. It'd been a while but I was ready to handle a fight. In fact, I think I needed one just to clear my head.

I sat down and nursed a coffee and a double glazed at Tim Horton's. A couple of goofball punks recognized me as the drummer from GIGB and said something about how hot our music sounded.

I told them to leave me alone or else I'd waste them. And that was the end of that.

16

The Set-Up

I knew that the whole music thing was down the tubes. Good Idea Gone Bad was dead. I was back to bashing a snare drum in my bedroom or sitting around with my headphones on just stewing over what might have been. I tried phoning Dariana plenty of times but she wasn't there and either her mother wasn't in the mood to take a message or her father just told me that I shouldn't phone so much because he was waiting for some business calls.

I felt really out of it at school so I cut a couple of days. The first day I walked around Halifax but the place didn't feel like home. I had an attitude and I was looking for trouble. When I passed the convenience store owned by the Lebanese family, I thought again about busting in the window or doing something serious. I thought it might cure me, but then I figured, what's the point? Why waste the energy? I just kept on walking.

The second day, I just stayed home and holed up in my room, watching dopey game shows on TV.

Some of the babes were cute but other than that it was a waste. I was beginning to wish I'd never joined up with Dariana and Alex. It was their fault I felt like this. They had let me down. Even Dariana — the one person in the world I really cared about, the only girl who ever really got through to me. What a loser she turned out to be.

Late that afternoon the doorbell rang. My mom was out shopping. I went downstairs figuring that whoever it was, I'd give him a hard time. Paper boy, maybe, or a salesman. I'd make him wish he hadn't picked my house.

It was Dariana.

"Hi," she said.

"Wassup?"

"Thought we should talk."

"Right."

She shrugged. "Well, it's more than that. Thought we should go somewhere together."

"Why?"

"I want to show you something."

"Like?"

"Like you have to come with me. You'll see."

"Where are we going?"

"I want you to meet some people."

"Like a party?"

"Not exactly."

"Exactly what, then?"

She didn't answer. So I gave it up. We were starting to sound like those contestants on the stupid game shows. Instead, we walked. She led — I followed — all the way to Gottingen Street

118

where we came to a crowd of kids hanging out in front of the drugstore.

"Guys, this is Mick," she said introducing me to a pretty low-life looking bunch of kids. I didn't know their names but I'd seen them around. They lived on and off the street but mostly on. This was a mixed crowd — every colour, every persuasion. It made me feel kind of itchy to get out of there.

Then I saw the guy I least wanted to see.

"I think you know Stephen," Dariana said.

"Yo," I said.

"How ya doing, Mick?"

The guy reached out to shake my hand. No way. I pulled my hand back. I grabbed onto my wrist. The damn watch. I was still wearing the creep's watch. I pulled my sleeve down over it. What was this supposed to be, some kind of guilt trip?

I felt the walls go up. I didn't want to deal with these people. What was Dariana trying to prove? "What are we doing here?" I demanded. "You don't want to hang out with these losers."

The other kids were staring at me now. And I was glaring back at them. Yeah, they knew who I was and who I hung out with. I wasn't sure, but maybe I'd trashed more than just Stephen here in the past. I never thought much of the weirdos who made their living on the street. Dave and me had our fun jerking them around on occasion.

Dariana didn't answer. Instead, one of her girl-friends did — some chick with heavy black eye make-up and spiked hair. She obviously thought she'd be tough, be cool, by giving me a hard time. "Yeah, Dariana, why *did* you bring this doorknob down here?"

The other kids laughed. Man, I hate being laughed at. If these guys weren't careful, I was going to smash some faces.

Stephen saw me clenching my fists. He knew what I was all about. He'd had the unfortunate luck to catch me at a bad moment before. "It's okay, Mick," he said. "You don't need to be afraid of us."

That just about did it. The volcano was ready to cut loose. The turkey was trying to prove he wasn't afraid of me. I was thinking that I'd correct that notion.

Dariana was tugging me away, though. "Relax, Mick. I just wanted you to meet some of my friends. I didn't say they were going to move in with you."

When we were away from there, I wanted an explanation. "Why would you want to hang out with a bunch of losers like that? Those people are worthless. They've got nothing. They're worth nothing. A bunch of freaks and fruits and ... they're not like us."

Dariana stopped dead in her tracks and grabbed onto my arm. "That was your last chance, Mick. I was really hoping that you'd changed. Just a little. I thought there was hope. I really wanted to believe that you were human underneath all that tough-guy stuff. But I was wrong. You're still stubborn and pig-headed. Even the music didn't teach you anything. Goodbye."

Maybe I should have just let her walk. It was hard to believe I let her push me that far and not react. Then, as I watched her walk away, I started thinking that she had been the only really good thing in my life. She had led me to something in music that I had never had before. I had this feeling that if she walked, everything walked. For good.

"Wait," I said running after her. "*What is it you want out of me, anyway?*" I pleaded. I wanted Dariana to ... to, well, care. And maybe she did, even then, because I listened while she told me all the things about myself that had been turning in my brain for the past weeks — ever since the cemetery, ever since the dance, maybe ever since the night we beat up Stephen. It was like she could read me — my past, my present, who knows, maybe my future.

I would have done anything for Dariana at that moment. And I did. I went back and apologized to all of them. "Sorry," I said to Stephen and the others who were still standing there. "Real sorry." But I didn't look straight at anyone.

"Now that you've left such a good impression on them, I think we can go," Dariana said. "We've got another stop."

She was holding my hand now and leading me down the block. I turned around to see if the others were watching. They were. They were all just standing there. All except for Stephen. He was starting to follow us. The guy didn't seem to know when to give it up.

Dariana led me to a pawn shop called Honest John's. Inside, the place was crammed with all kinds of music gear. Gretch and Fender guitars were hanging from the walls. Marshall amps were stacked up on the floor and a couple of dismantled drum sets were scattered around. Behind the glass counter was a bald guy with a hearing aid.

"John, this is my friend, Mick."

John looked up and smiled. "It's good to see you, Dariana. How are things at home?"

"They've been worse," she answered. "What about you? How's business?"

"Always the same," John answered, putting a finger to his ear to adjust the volume on his hearing aid.

The little bell rang as the door opened again. I turned around to discover that Stephen had followed us here. I shook my head in disbelief.

John smiled at Stephen. He swept his hand around the roomful of musical chaos. "Look around, kids," he said. "It's all for sale. Try out anything that looks interesting." Then he turned away and fiddled with a pile of cameras on the counter.

That's when I began to realize I'd been tricked. Stephen had picked up a Fender Stratocaster and plugged it into an amp. He hit a couple of chords, tuned a string and then cranked up the overdrive on the amplifier. I walked away towards the back of the store, pretending I wasn't interested.

It all came back to me. We had been goofing around in front of the library when Stephen stopped by with his acoustic guitar and started to jam to my trash-can drums. And then the guys grounded him. We never gave him a chance to play.

I tried to ignore him. I tried to ignore both of them. But Dariana had plugged an old Yamaha keyboard into another amp and was hitting some chords.

Now I was beginning to get the picture.

"No way!" I shouted at her. "Not in a million years."

Dariana pretended she didn't hear me. I looked at John. I think he had just turned his hearing aid off. He didn't seem to be paying attention to any of us, despite the noise. I was standing in the pawn shop of the deaf. I wanted out of there.

I walked past Dariana and Stephen just as they were starting to get in sync. I walked out of there onto the sidewalk of Gottingen Street. But just as I was walking out the door, Dariana started to sing something and I immediately recognized the song. Even without a mike, her voice came on powerful and full of impact. She was singing "Daredevil Difference," the first song of hers I ever heard, the first one I had jammed on when Good Idea Gone Bad was beginning to exist.

I stood there, outside the pawn shop, staring at the cars going by in the afternoon sun. I stood there listening to her voice. And then the guitar lead came on strong. Man, she was a shrewd one, this music lady. Was this whole scene really a set-up?

Stephen's guitar came up loud and wailing. It blasted out of the pawn shop onto the street. Backed by the keyboard chords, it gave a wild, haunting shriek that stabbed like an ice pick into my brain. I wanted to turn and walk away but I didn't move. The guitar notes zapped like lightning through my skull, reminding me of the not-so-old but dead-and-gone days of Good Idea Gone Bad, and also reminding me of all the great metal bands I'd ever heard. It was a hard, powerful and overwhelming sound that flowed out onto the street. It was full of pride and hurt and outrage and courage and anger all at once.

When Dariana started singing again, there was some perfect melting of voice and shrill overdrive guitar that just about made my socks crawl down into my shoes.

Suddenly from my right, some old geezer came storming out of the drugstore and pushed past me into Honest John's. I turned around and saw him screaming something at Stephen, then screaming at John. But John must have hosted his share of heavy metal talent in his store before. When the music got loud, he just turned his hearing aid down to dead-end deaf and soaked up the serenity. So, when the drugstore dude started screaming, "No more noise, John. No more of this horrible noise!" John just smiled and went back to his cameras on the counter.

The dude was still screaming, "No more noise!" when I walked back in there. There was a selection of drum sticks on the counter. I picked out a pair, looked for something handy to bash. The drum parts were scattered and I didn't see anything easy to get at. But there was a big plastic trash can by the door. I had to move the music critic out of the way to get to it. Then I turned it over and I started to play. Dariana did another verse. Stephen took the cue for an extended lead riff and eventually the drugstore guy couldn't stand it any more. He retreated back to his store.

When the tune was over, I turned the trash can upright and I set the sticks back on the counter.

Dariana and Stephen had a look on them like they had just finished a sold-out performance at the Toronto Skydome. But then Stephen set the guitar down, turned off the amp and cleared his throat. "Well, I guess I gotta get moving," he said, trying to sound really nonchalant. "Anybody got the time?"

"Yeah, man," I said, undoing the Van Halen watch from my wrist and handing it to him. "I got the time. Here you go."

17

Knees Like Jelly, Arms Like Rubber

We hadn't been practising for more than a month when Barry told us there was a gig coming up that we couldn't turn down. "There's going to be this rally on Gottingen Street," he said. "Kind of like a big block party to bring people together and make a stand against violence in the city. It's being put together by a whole bunch of community groups."

"You mean fruits, feminists and flakes?" I asked.

Barry shook his head. "You rather we party with the PFMM?"

I held my drumsticks in the air. "Hey, I wasn't complaining. A gig's a gig. I just wanted to make sure I knew who I was working for."

I looked at Stephen. The guy was actually laughing at my joke. We were getting along pretty good considering our past history. It worried me sometimes that I didn't hate him like I used to. But I tried not to let it get to me. We played music. The three of us were good. Good Idea Gone Bad had just gone a little weirder, that's all.

"It's getting worse, isn't it?" Dariana asked Barry.

"What do you mean?"

"More beatings," she said, looking very serious all of a sudden. "Little kids getting punched around at school. Kids on the street getting swarmed. More fights between black and white gangs. Is it just 'cause I'm paying attention or is it worse?"

Dariana was in *very* serious mood. The girl actually sat around thinking about this stuff. She probably guessed that I sometimes missed being part of the downtown action. I really felt like bashing someone once in a while. Even music couldn't take all my energy.

So here we were — three people with problems who had become a loud and angry band with something to sing about. Stephen had never really fit in anywhere — for the obvious reason. Dariana had been at odds with the world since the day she was born. And I don't exactly know how to describe my problem. It seemed that I was always really ticked off about something.

"Yeah," Barry said. "It's worse. You see it in the news. Heck, you see it on the street. Women are afraid to go out at night. Parents are afraid to let their kids walk down the street. You got white kids picking on black kids. Blacks picking on

Whites. Men stalking women. Gay-bashing. It didn't used to be that way around here."

"Hey, let's not get all nostalgic for the sixties again," I told him. I hated it when Barry slipped off into his good-old-days routine.

Barry pretended he didn't hear me. "So what's the story? Are we in or out? You guys want the gig or not?"

"How much we getting paid?" I asked. I was a pro, right? I should know how much it was worth.

"The place will be crawling with media people. We're talking about twenty thousand dollars worth of free publicity here," Barry said.

"In other words, we don't get paid, Mick," Stephen said.

"That's fine with me," Dariana said. "I think the whole capitalist thing sucks anyway. We don't need the money."

Now Dariana was putting down money. Everyday it was a new twist with her. It was hard to keep my head adjusted to it.

"I bet that if we don't do this gig, they got no one, right?"

"Wrong," Barry said. "Mind Over Matter is interested if you guys aren't ready to do it."

Mind over Matter was Alex's new band, the one managed by Giles, the band so clean they were being groomed for big success. "Okay, we'll do it," I conceded. I knew it was a lost cause from the beginning. "Who could turn down twenty thousand dollars worth of free publicity?"

For the big event they closed off a couple of blocks of Gottingen. It had a pretty neat feel to it with no cars, just people filling the street. We had our gear set up on the back of a flatbed trailer that acted as a stage and Barry borrowed a serious sound system for the event.

Around the perimeter of the crowd were cops. I'd never seen so many police in one place, but I'd given up worrying every time I saw a cop. If they wanted me, they would have hauled me in long ago. Besides, sometimes I convinced myself I was a changed person, and today I was on the side of the good guys. Maybe the cops didn't trust the organizers of this thing. Maybe they didn't trust the crowd. With this many people on the street in this part of town, anything could happen.

Before we could play, we had to listen to a bunch of speeches by some people who thought they could fix all the problems of the city by just standing up and talking them all away. The first one to take the mike was this skinny old babe name Maude something who talked like she'd been a radical feminist since the 1920s. That was a bit much for me to handle. Next, a black minister gave a little preachy thing about standing up to injustice. He reminded me of somebody I'd seen in a rap video. The audience was this really crazy mix of black and white people, street life and university types, mothers with little kids, Ozzie and Harriet suburbanites and high school kids from all over town. The whole time the speakers were hogging the mikes, I kept thinking that this was going to be one very tough audience.

The crowd was so big, I couldn't see the back of it. I kept looking at the faces and trying to figure what sort of music each one listened to. Rap for this one. Barry Manilow for that one. k.d. lang for that one over there. There was probably an infestation of sixties folkheads in the crowd as well. Man, we didn't have *anything* for any of them. All we had was our stuff — it was new, it was raw and it was loud. Thinking about it made me nervous.

I saw Stephen talking to some of his old street friends. A few of them gave me the creeps. Suddenly I felt somebody squeeze my hand. It was Dariana and she was smiling at me. She'd been real intent on listening to the speakers but now she was paying attention to me. "I'm really glad we're doing this," she told me. "I'm glad we're doing this together."

"Me too," I said. "We'll blow them all away."

Another speaker came up to the podium, somebody who said he was from the Halifax Peace Society. I wasn't paying too much attention to him. In fact, I was thinking about Dariana. I felt like that invisible barrier between us had finally broken down. I wanted to tell her that. I wanted to try to tell her how I really felt about her — not just how much I respected her music but how much I cared for her. But I knew that as soon as I opened my mouth I would sound like an idiot.

Just then, Alex arrived on the scene with some of his band. He walked right up to us, dressed in clothes that must have cost a couple of hundred bucks.

"Hi Slick," Dariana said. "Good to see you." The babe didn't hold any grudges. I couldn't be that polite with this turkey who had punked out on us.

"I'm glad you guys are doing this show," Alex said. "It's your style."

"What do you mean?" I asked. I could detect a put-down when I heard it.

"They asked us first," Alex said, "but Giles thought it was a little too sensitive so we turned them down."

I got the picture loud and clear. But I didn't believe him, the little snot.

"Besides, we've got a plane to catch later this afternoon. It's our first studio session in T.O. D and D signed us on."

"Congratulations," Dariana told Alex, pretending she really cared. Dariana was squeezing my hand harder. She knew that it might look bad for me to punch the guy's lights out or rip his tongue out of his mouth, right there in front of everybody at the anti-violence rally.

"Yeah, congratulations," I told Alex.

"How's the new guitar player working out?" Alex asked, pointing over towards Stephen. One of his other band buddies beside him was whispering something and all three of them were cracking up.

"You know how it is breaking in a new musician," Dariana said, sounding very professional. "It's tough at first and then things click."

I couldn't wait until Alex heard just how good his replacement was. But I wasn't going to say what was on my mind. I just said, "You'll have to excuse us. We gotta get ready to do some music."

The speeches were winding down. We pulled Stephen away from his friends and walked back behind the flatbed trailer stage.

"Do you really think they asked Alex's band first?" I asked Dariana.

"It doesn't matter," Stephen said.

"But I wanna know," I said. Up until then I had been hanging onto my confidence. Now it was slipping down to my knees.

The final speaker was finishing up and I knew we were about to be introduced. Why was it so important to me whether we were asked first or not?

"I don't know," Dariana answered. "I honestly don't. But it doesn't matter. We've been wanting an audience for a long time. Now we've got it. And it's a big one. You think I'm not nervous, too?"

Whoa. She had come out and said it. She had read me like a book. That's what I was feeling. I was just looking for excuses but the truth was I wasn't just nervous. I was shaking-in-my-boots scared. I'd never felt like this before. This was completely different. I didn't know if I could go on.

I listened to the lady on the stage introducing us. "And now a band that shares our concerns for making these streets safe. You know them for their underground hits like 'The Condom Song' and 'Daredevil Difference.' Here they are — Good Idea Gone Bad!"

My knees felt like jelly and my arms like rubber as I walked out onto the stage and sat down at the drums. In front of us was a sea of faces. People were clapping and cheering but the crowd scared me. I felt like they were all my enemies.

I knew it was up to me to get the beat going, to start hammering and get the music moving. I couldn't see whether Stephen was scared or not because he had his back to me. But I caught the look on Dariana's face. It told me that she felt the same way I did.

The clapping had subsided. People were waiting for something to happen. For a split second I felt frozen, immobile. *What if I really mucked this up for good?* said that voice of doubt inside my head. I closed my eyes and tried to pretend I was back in Dariana's garage. It wasn't working.

But then I heard one single note coming from Dariana's keyboard. She was holding down one key. The sound of that one note was like electricity connecting us. It was like some powerful, insistent force recharging all the batteries of my will. Stephen joined in now with the first thunderous chord of "Downtown Dangerous" and I felt the energy double. I felt the connection between all three of us and suddenly my arms were

133

moving. My eyes were still closed, my head tilted up to the sky but I was in motion. I was letting the rhythm of my drums take over as we launched into the intro for the song.

With the monster PA system it sounded like an avalanche of sound. I heard each drum beat echo off the walls of the storefronts. I opened my eyes as Dariana began to sing the first verse and I saw the sea of faces again. But this time it wasn't like they were my enemies. They were all my friends.

We roared, we wailed, we made music that must have shaken the foundations of the buildings. Dariana's voice was strong and her songs were angry. Her anger was an anger of caring. I listened to her words again and knew for sure that the organizers had asked us first. Dariana's songs were right in sync with this anti-violence thing. We were now the centre of all that energy. As I watched Stephen launch into space with his magnificent lead guitar work, the irony of the moment came back to haunt me. And when I looked past him out into the crowd, I saw Alex watching, knowing that we'd replaced him with someone better. That made me feel good and I knew that I really didn't care how different Stephen was. I didn't care if he was a Martian with three heads. He was in the band and he was one of us.

There were other faces now in the crowd that I recognized, other faces that I wish I had never known. Dave, Roach and Lanker were bullying their way from the outside fringe right up towards the stage.

They looked out of place here — these three ugly goons with black leather jackets, metal-toed workboots and monster bad attitudes — Lanker with his newly shaved head, Roach with his creepy sunglasses and Dave with the hate just screaming out from his repulsive face. Just looking at them made me realize how different I was from what I'd been. But then I realized that something was different about them as well. They were here in broad daylight. They weren't just sneaking away from some crime in the night. They had come down here for a purpose and they weren't just there for the music.

18

At Home among the Weirdos

After about forty-five minutes, we took our break as planned. I had a kind of glow on from the thrill of the clapping and cheering from the crowd. GIGB had finally and truly gone public and we were a smashing hit.

I came down from the stage with my head buzzing to find my old buddies waiting for me. "We gotta talk," Dave said to me, never sounding more polite or friendly, though his face said something different.

"I don't think I want to talk right now."

"Don't worry," Roach said. "It's cool. We just have some news we wanted to share. Good news."

So I followed them to the end of the trailer and away from the stage. We sat down on some crates. Dariana watched us. She looked worried and with good reason.

"I can't believe you got a fruitcake like that playing guitar with you," Lanker said, rubbing his hand across his shaved head that had just a tiny amount of stubble trying to grow back in.

"He's good isn't he?" I said.

Lanker sucked in his breath and shook his head.

I think the guys were testing me. I think they had a hard time believing I was no longer one of them. With their own perverse sense of loyalty, I think they wanted to believe that deep down I was still one of them.

"You remember how you used to say that we should do some real damage to that Lebanese store?" Dave said.

"I remember."

"Foreigners come over here stealing all the jobs, man," Roach said. "It's not right."

Roach had never even tried to get a job, even a part-time one. And I don't even think his old man had done a day's work or ever wanted to.

"Gotta show 'em a lesson, right?" Dave pointed out.

"So we kicked in the window the other night. Stole some cigs and stuff. You shoulda been there."

Lanker pulled out his wallet. He pulled out a fistful of dollars. "And look at this. Ripped it off some Paki kid in Clayton Park last night."

"Like taking candy from a baby." Roach was all smiles behind his shades.

"Point is, Mick, you're missing out on all the fun. And we feel sorta bad. We've been through a lot together. We thought we should give you another chance." Dave was serious. I think he actually did feel sorry for me. Or maybe he had chosen to ignore the GIGB lyrics and liked the idea of having an up-and-coming rockmeister as part of his crowd. Their idea of fun, though, now sounded stupid and cruel to me.

"She got to you, didn't she?" Dave asked.

Yeah, I wanted to say. She did get to me. The music got to me. I *was* different. There was no going back. But this wasn't the time for lectures.

"You guys are too much," I said smiling. "I'm really glad you came to hear the music."

I left them with their jaws unhinged and walked back to the stage.

I felt much cooler, much more together when I sat back down at my drums for the second set. Meeting with my old cronies didn't even faze me.

I looked over my shoulder to see what the guys would do next. A couple of cops were talking to them. It looked like they were hassling Dave.

"Ready?" Dariana asked me.

"No," I said. I nodded towards my old friends. They were surrounded by six cops in total now. They were being led out front, out through the crowd and away from the stage. People pulled back as they were led through. I didn't understand it. We had just been talking. I knew that they hadn't done anything wrong. Not *today* anyway. I watched as one patrolman grabbed for Dave's shoulder and pushed him along. Dave tried to jerk away from him and Lanker reached over to take the cop's hand off his chum.

When I saw two of the cops pull out their night sticks, I had to react. This was all wrong. I knew exactly why Dave, Lanker and Roach were being hassled right now. It wasn't anything they had done. It was because they looked bad, they looked tough and they *looked like* they might cause trouble.

But no one had a right to kick somebody out of here just because of the way they looked.

I jumped down from the stage and made my way through the crowd to where the action was.

Maybe because I was part of the band and since I had been on stage, the police couldn't just ignore me when I demanded, "Why are you pushing them around? They have a right to be here."

Three cops now had sticks in their hands. They looked good and ready to use them. Another patrolmen was eyeing me. I had this weird feeling that they knew who we were ... they knew what we had all done.

"Get those creeps out of here," someone in the crowd yelled. "They're troublemakers. They have no right to be here!"

The absurdity of that idiot shouting these words hit me like slap in the face. Why weren't Dave, Lanker and Roach allowed to be here at this rally? Why should they have to leave? Was this event only for the privileged who *looked* normal?

"These are my friends," I said to the police. "I invited them backstage. I want them to stay."

I knew it was a gamble. I knew the cops had good reason to worry about these three being here. But they were here and that was something. Maybe one of Dariana's songs would get to them. Maybe something about these people getting together to say "no more violence" would mean something. But if they were booted out of here now ... well, I know exactly how I would feel. I'd be madder than before.

"Sorry, son," one of the policemen said to me. "These guys are trouble." They began to push them away. And Dave had the look on his face, the look that said he'd let someone, even a cop, push him only so far.

Dariana and Stephen had followed me off the stage. They were beside me now. Everybody in the crowd knew that something was going on.

"Let them stay!" Dariana shouted at the cops. But they weren't listening. More police were moving in now. What they saw was a flashpoint, some serious trouble about to break out.

"Come on, man," Stephen said, grabbing onto the sleeve of one of the uniforms. "You don't have to kick them out of here."

I don't think the cop got a good look at Stephen. He just knew that someone had grabbed him and he wasn't going to wait and see what happened next. He turned and swung his night stick. Stephen saw it coming. He was quick. He ducked out of the way but ended up falling on the ground.

"No!" screamed Dariana. Lanker and Dave were trying to get away. The cops were trying to hold onto them. Roach was down on the ground covering his head like he expected to get it next. Some of Stephen's friends were pushing through the crowd coming to help him. They started to push the cops away from Stephen and the police were pushing back. People were shoving, everybody was starting to freak and I knew that in a few seconds someone was going to get hurt.

I quickly backed away and jumped up on stage. I grabbed the microphone from the stand and looked over to Barry at the soundboard. Gave him a thumb in the air. He knew I wanted the volume fully cranked.

"Okay," I said, breathlessly into the mike, making maybe the first speech I ever made in my life. "Everybody be cool." The words reverberated off the buildings. "Just everybody be cool."

I guess I was loud enough to make everyone take notice. I had their attention now. I looked over towards the disturbance. Lanker and Dave had their arms twisted up behind them. A couple of Stephen's friends were squared off in front of two cops with night sticks. Roach was still somewhere down on the ground, I guessed, cowering. And Dariana was right there in the middle of it. If I couldn't say the right thing, somebody would get hurt. Maybe just a face in the crowd or maybe it would be Dariana.

"It's all a misunderstanding," I said. I was looking at the cops but I was talking to everyone. "It's not right to throw my friends out of here. They came here like everybody else did and they have

141

a right to be here. They're being picked on because they look like they don't fit in."

The crowd was almost quiet, but people were all jammed up around the police. People were taking sides.

"Everybody just back off," I said. "Yeah, just back off, okay?"

"How about it?" I said, looking at the patrolmen, then around at the crowd. "Back off. Please."

I saw one of the policemen looking at me. He turned to the others, nodded. They backed off. Roach got up off the ground. Lanker, Dave and Roach were standing there with everybody watching them. That was the moment I knew I had made the biggest gamble of my life. Maybe Dave would bust someone. Maybe Lanker would think it was a great chance to turn the whole scene into a riot. Or maybe Roach would spit at one of the cops and then run for it.

Instead, someone else in the crowd yelled out, "Let 'em stay!"

"Yeah, that's right," someone else shouted. "Let everyone stay. This is our party, right? And everyone's invited."

A few people clapped and cheered but a lot of people were just plain confused as to what was going on. When things got quiet, I saw Stephen and Dariana coming back up to the stage. Somebody helped both of them hop up on the front.

But I caught a glimpse of Dave. I saw that old familiar hate on his face. He put his hands to his mouth and shouted something at me — something loud, angry and full of the same old hate. "Forget it, Mick. We don't *want* to stay. We don't want to hang out with a bunch of wimps and weirdos. You can all go to hell as far as I'm concerned."

But no one shouted back anything at them. I watched as Lanker, Roach and Dave weaved towards the back of the crowd and found their way out of there on their own. The cops let them be.

Dariana was hitting a chord again. I felt a twinge of loss as I stumbled back to my drum set, tripping over one of the power cords. I wondered if we had just won or lost a battle. I wondered if any of this had meant anything at all.

Dariana launched us into "Daredevil Difference" and it all came back to me — the early days. The way I used to be. I knew I could never go back. I knew I had changed and I was hoping that sooner or later something good would happen for Roach, Dave and Lanker, and then they would change too. Maybe. That's what I hoped for as I sat there and played my heart out on my drums in front of those people on Gottingen Street in Halifax.

After the concert, I felt oddly at home among the weirdos, the fruits, the feminists and everybody else who kept telling us what a wonderful gig we played. Stephen introduced me to a couple of his gay friends and I acted like it was no big deal even though I still felt really uncomfortable and wouldn't let them get too friendly.

Dariana introduced me to the old grey-haired babe who had given one of the speeches. "Mick, this is Maude."

I nodded. I took her to be the kind of feminist who had started this whole business of making things difficult for guys like me, you know, who wanted to have a traditional relationship with a girl.

"You're a good man, Mick," she said. "I admire you for what you did. And I like your music, too."

Oh, right, like I really believed her. But Dariana was watching me. It was another one of her tests. I wanted to pass this one. I truly did.

I pointed my drumsticks straight at the woman. "The way I figure it, lady, it goes like this. We're all different in some way or another. And it really doesn't matter. We just gotta do what we gotta do and learn to live with everybody else."

She gave me a hug just then and I was caught off-guard. She was old and she was skinny and I felt her thin, boney arms pulled tight around me with a kind of strength that shocked me. When she let me go, she playfully hit me hard on the arm with her knuckle. "Keep it up," she told me, then turned and walked away.

Stephen's friends were laughing at me. I guess I looked pretty bewildered. That's when Dariana slipped an arm around me and said, "I think it went pretty well."

"Yeah," I said. "Twenty thousand dollars worth of free publicity. I think we scored big." But I knew what she meant. I just didn't have the words in me right then to tell her what I had finally figured out.

"Let's go find something to eat. I'm starving," she said.

"Me too. But I'm broke."

"I'm buying," Dariana said. "Let's stash the gear in the garage and then I'll take you out to dinner."

"This isn't like a date or anything?" I asked.

"No way," she said, the sweet smile on her face telling me the opposite. "You think I'd go out on a date with a big ugly goof like you?"

And I knew then that it was the beginning of something very fine. A good idea had just become a whole lot better.

Afterword

When I opened the mail today, I came across an offer from Time-Life Books — "a unique chance to probe the twisted minds and deeds of America's most violent criminals." If I simply returned the card that already had my name and address printed on it, Time-Life would send me my own free examination copy of the first of a series of books about murderers and other violent criminals. My free book would be about serial killers. (Up until a couple of years ago, I didn't even know what a serial killer was.) I could tell from the promo literature that the book would be full of plenty of colour photographs and descriptive text with many details.

Was I interested in the offer? *No way.*

In fact, I was pretty angry about it. Somebody was about to make a million bucks (or much more) by capitalizing on human misfortune, by catering to the lowest instincts of entertainment and by ultimately helping to popularize and glorify violence in our society. And the worst part, perhaps, is that I knew this book would find plenty of readers, make lots of money and help to bump what I might call "good" books further down the list of books read in anyone's lifetime.

Violence in any form sucks. Once when I was a kid, I had my head bashed into the windscreen of a car until blood ran down my face. I had just finished playing a gig with a band named Prodigy at a Friday night dance. I had tried to stop one guy from punching out the lights of another guy who had said the wrong thing at the wrong time. As a result, I got hammered by someone who had obviously spent a lot more time practising with his fists than I had.

Good Idea Gone Bad is a book about music — the alternative music scene in Halifax — but it is also about violence. Given my complaint against Time-Life, you might wonder, why is this guy who is opposed to violence writing a book where the main character is a racist thug who gets his jollies by bashing anyone he sees as "different?" Isn't there already too much violence in the movies and on TV and even in books?

The answer is yes and no.

Yes, most of the violence you see in the media is there for shock and entertainment value. And it still sucks. There's no doubt in my mind that it helps to increase violence in the real world. And I'll never write an account of a mass murderer in book form simply because, supposedly, "that's what the public wants."

The reason I explored violence in this book is because I was interested in examining the root of violence both in myself and in the world around me. That's what *Good Idea Gone Bad* is all about.

It was a rough book to write. Mick was a difficult character for me to get into. In order to write a good novel, to some degree I have to become the character who is telling the story. So imagine for a minute what happens when this author become Mick.

Several times in my life, I've actively worked to stop wars, to get rid of nuclear weapons, to promote gun control, to reduce violence on TV, and to counter racial hatred. If you read any of my other books, you'll find that there's a strong underlying theme of "tolerance." Everyone should get along with everyone else no matter how different they are. I'm a pacifist, too, which means that I think all forms of fighting — schoolyard and battleground — are stupid. I'll do what I can to end violence.

So figure this: somewhere inside of the complex of personalities that is me, Mick exists. I think there's a little bit of Mick in you as well, no matter how freaky that sounds.

Intolerant tough guys hate others — immigrants, "fags and feminists," racial minorities — because of basic insecurities, frustration and an anger that grows from a very primary fear. We all share some of that insecurity and the fear that goes along with it. Most people don't act out the violence that results from it, but some do.

Having written from Mick's point of view, I think I understand the problem a little bit better.

If Mick remained the same stubborn, pig-headed bully that he was at the beginning of this chain of events, there would have been no story here. Fiction, though, is created around characters and the changes they go through. Mick is a different drummer by the end of the book and therein lies the tale.

But I wasn't writing a book exclusively about violence. I was also writing a book about music. The same night that I had my head bashed in while trying to stop a fight, I had just had a great session playing lead guitar in my band in front of a crowd of a couple of hundred kids. We had played our hearts out. We wailed and thrashed and sang and stomped and jammed away until everybody's ears rang and neighbours were complaining that we were disturbing the peace. But when we had to stop at the end of the gig, we knew we had succeeded in making the music work through our drums, guitars and keyboard, and through us as well. Maybe that's why I had felt invincible and had to be brought back to cold, hard reality by a guy who did his communicating with fists instead of guitar picks.

I like to think that I haven't lost the music. I still play guitar. I've just recorded a couple of songs adapting poetry to music. A pair of videos are in the works. So, when Dariana, Mick and Alex work out a new tune, I'm there with them at the heart of the musical creative process. You may not have heard of Good Idea Gone Bad as a band yet, but I guarantee you, their history is being lived out in some variation of this story in garages and basements around Halifax (currently the hottest new music centre in the country) and around the world.

The music and the message that Mick and Dariana create is inextricably entwined. The songs have sound but they also have lyrics with real content. As sometimes happens with books, original music with real lyric content is often the first to get condemned, to get censored, to get banned. Maybe someone will even want to attack this novel for its violence, for its language or because Mick is not a respectable character. Maybe it should be kept out of the schools because it deals with subjects too sensitive to be discussed.

If that were to happen, I think that we'd all be losing something. We'd be closing our eyes to the root of the problems. We'd be giving over the power of influence to Time-Life with their gaudy books on serial killers, mass murderers, as well as to all the TV and movie producers who glorify the death and destruction that has become so much of our public and private lives.

Lesley Choyce,
Lawrencetown Beach, Nova Scotia
September 1, 1993

AGMV
MARQUIS
Québec, Canada
1998